Nose-down in a pil... conclusion that I r... greatest skier after... on about placing ou... the slope – didn't he... stay upright, let alone remember geometry lessons?

Also by Mary Hooper

Cassie
Janey's Diary
Janey's Summer
Lexie
Making Waves
Short Cut to Love
School Friends 1: First Term
School Friends 2: Star
School Friends 4: The Boys Next Door

MARY HOOPER

School Friends 3

PARK WOOD ON ICE

MAMMOTH

First published in Great Britain 1991
by Mammoth, an imprint of Mandarin Paperbacks
Michelin House, 81 Fulham Road, London SW3 6RB

Mandarin is an imprint of the Octopus Publishing Group

Text copyright © 1991 Mary Hooper

ISBN 0 7497 0594 9

A CIP catalogue record for this title
is available from the British Library

Typeset by Falcon Typographic Art Ltd,
Edinburgh & London
Printed in Great Britain
by Cox & Wyman Ltd, Reading, Berkshire

Contents

Chapter One
FRIDAY: OFF WE GO!

'Hold still!' Mum said. 'I want to do up your anorak.'

'Don't keep calling it an anorak,' I said irritably – well, it was five o'clock in the morning. 'It doesn't look like an ordinary old anorak, does it? It's supposed to be a skiing jacket.'

I broke away from her and studied myself anxiously in the hall mirror. My salopettes were a brilliantly shiny emerald green, and the skiing jacket that was supposed to match was emerald green without the brilliantly shiny bit. Mum had seen it in a camping shop at half the price of a proper one, and insisted that no one would notice.

'Of course it doesn't look like an ordinary old anorak,' Mum said smoothly, 'it's a perfect match. No one will ever know that it was bought separately.'

'I don't know . . .' I said, examining it worriedly.

'Well, it's wear that or not go at all,' she said briskly.

I yawned and turned away from the mirror. It would have to do.

'Anyway, it would only be someone like Araminta who'd notice,' Mum said, 'and I thought you said she wasn't going.'

'I don't think she is,' I said. 'She's supposed to get up to date with *Village Life* episodes in the holidays.' I yawned again. 'Why do we have to go so early, d'you think?'

'To catch the early ferry and get a good start on the French roads before the weekend traffic.' It was then Mum's turn to look anxious. 'I do hope the driver remembers to drive on the right-hand side,' she said. 'Dad had terrible trouble; I had to tie a red ribbon on the wing mirror to remind him.'

'Well, if he forgets I'll bellow down the coach and tell him,' I said.

'Don't do that!' she said, alarmed. 'You might break his concentration.'

'I was *joking*, Mum.'

8

She checked over my case, my shoulder-bag, my packet of sandwiches and my bag with my passport in it and ticked them off on her fingers, muttering under her breath. 'Now, have you got everything?' she said.

'You should know,' I pointed out. 'You've done all the packing.'

'Yes, well . . . I couldn't trust you, could I?'

'Isn't anyone else going to get up and see me off?' I asked, niggled. Here was I, venturing into foreign parts for the first time; why weren't my dad and my brothers standing at the door waving flags of all nations?

'Ha!' Mum said. 'That'll be the day. I'll go and get the car out.'

I looked at Mum critically as we drove down the road: she was wearing a hundred-year-old pink track suit over her nightie, had no make-up on and her hair was sticking out all over the place. 'You're not going to get out of the car when we get to school, are you?' I asked cautiously.

'Of course I am,' she said. 'I want to see you safely on to the coach and I'd like to see your friends.'

'You've seen them all on TV,' I said. 'That's enough, isn't it?'

'I hardly saw them at all!' she objected.

'All I saw was quite a lot about whats-her-name? Araminta Eversage.'

'*Jane*,' I said. 'Most of us call her Jane.'

Jane – or Araminta Eversage if you wanted to keep in with her – had a part in a soap called *Village Life* and was in our class at Park Wood. At the end of last term the camera teams had descended on us and made a mini-documentary, *A Day in the Life of a Young Actress*, which had been shown a few weeks back. It had been quite exciting although the filming of it had driven Mrs Mackie, our form teacher, quite demented.

'All I'm saying is, if you want to get out of the car you'll have to go back and change first,' I said. I looked down at her feet and felt quite faint. 'Especially as you're wearing furry slippers!'

'So I am,' she said gaily.

The nearer we got to school the more excited I began to feel. I hadn't let myself before, just in case something happened at the last moment and I couldn't go, but now it was near enough to believe it. I was going to be brilliant at skiing – I was sure I was. Okay, I hadn't been too hot when I'd gone to the dry ski slope, but everyone said how much better and easier it was on real snow. And besides, I had to be good at *something* . . .

As we drove into the school playground the place looked really different, quite weird in the almost-darkness. The cars delivering girls still had their headlights on and there were two big coaches, one blue and one red, parked one each side of the playground with:

PARK WOOD SCHOOL SKIING TRIP written on their indicator boards.

I clutched Mum's arm. 'I'm really going!' I said.

'I should hope you are,' she said, 'you've cost me goodness knows how much in skiing equipment otherwise.' She looked at me severely. 'Now, you will be sensible, won't you? Don't take any risks . . . stay with the teachers all the time . . . don't overtire yourself . . . no staying up till all hours having midnight feasts.'

'No, no – of course not,' I said, jiggling in my seat and anxious to get away. 'I'd better be off, hadn't I? We're nearly late and the teachers will be wanting to count everyone.'

'Write then, love,' Mum said, 'and don't ever go out without those new vests I bought you. It's deceptive up on those mountains, you think it's sunny but . . .'

'Yes, yes!' I said, giving myself a mental reminder to leave the vests in the case and just screw them up so they looked worn. 'I'd better go, Mum. Bye!'

11

'How about a kiss?' she asked, putting on her fond-mummy face.

I leaned over and gave her one quickly. 'I'll write when I get there. See you soon!'

I got my case out of the back, held all my other bits under one arm and ran to the nearest, red, coach, which turned out to be full of second and third years. We first years – there were more of us – had the blue one to ourselves.

As I walked over to the blue coach I was horrified to see that Mum had disobeyed instructions and got out of the car, and was talking to Doris – Miss Harmer – the Headmistress, who'd come to see us off.

I sped past quickly, but not before Mum recognised me and shouted, 'It's all right – they change to French coaches and French drivers on the other side!'

'Oh good!' I said, and ran a bit faster and jumped on the blue coach. With a bit of luck no one would have realised that she belonged to me.

'Cases in the side!' the driver called – it was Mr Johnson, one of the miserable drivers who drove the school buses – so I dutifully got off, threw mine in the hold with all the others and got back on again.

I called excitedly to everyone on the coach;

they were in a rainbow mix of different coloured salopettes and ski jackets. The twins were in red, and both had the same haircuts, so we'd never tell them apart, Cerise had the brightest pink all-in-one suit I'd ever seen, Alison looked menacing in a black jacket, Annabel had a pale lilac designer outfit and Philippa, in her usual place beside her, matched her in purple. Mouse looked cute and suitably mouselike in grey with furry earmuffs and Alice, Erica, Donna and Su were all in different shades of blue. Everyone seemed to be there except Fleur.

I sat down on the seat nearest the door – which happened to be next to Cerise.

'You can't sit here,' she said. 'I'm keeping this place just in case Araminta turns up at the last minute.'

'I'm not staying here,' I said, 'I just want to look out for Fleur.'

'But if Araminta comes . . .'

'If Jane comes, I'll move,' I promised. 'But you don't really think she's going to turn up now, do you?'

'She said she'd try,' Cerise said. 'She said that if filming schedules could be changed . . .'

I grinned. Poor Cerise would be quite lost on this holiday without her precious star of a best friend.

13

Mrs Mackie climbed aboard; a practically unrecognisable Mrs Mackie with pom-pom hat, jeans and red skiing jacket.

'Morning, girls!' she called, and we all shouted good morning back. 'Are we all here?'

'Fleur's not!' I said, and Mrs Mackie said we could wait a few more minutes. We were joined by Miss Hermitage, our PE teacher, and Miss Lemming and Mrs Mullins – and were pleased to see nasty Mrs Taylor, Maths, going into the other coach. Mr Lloyd, our drama teacher, came in and settled himself with Miss Hermitage at the back, then a bit later Mrs Mackie said we really had to be going in case the traffic through London was bad and we missed the ferry.

'But what about Fleur?' I wailed.

'You can be *my* partner,' Cerise said to me comfortingly. 'And you can borrow my fluorescent face make-up.'

But this wasn't much consolation for not having Fleur. All the parents' cars flashed their headlights as we drove out of the school, and the coaches flashed back, but I didn't feel half as excited any more. It just wasn't going to be the same without my best friend. Whatever could have happened to her?

Ten minutes into the journey, when we

were on a dual carriageway, Mr Johnson started muttering to himself. I was still sitting at the front with Cerise and I could hear him: 'If the damn fool wants to pass me, why doesn't he go? What's he think he's playing at? Blasted weekend drivers!'

'Is there something the matter, Mr Johnson?' Mrs Mackie asked politely from behind.

'Yes – some blasted fool behind flashing his headlights non-stop,' the driver grumbled. 'Think they own the road!'

'Perhaps it's someone with a message,' Mrs Mackie suggested, and I suddenly got an idea, jumped out of my seat and ran to the back.

'No running round the coach!' Mrs Mackie called sternly, but I was kneeling up on the back seat by then and looking out, then waving and jumping up and down on the seat.

'It's Fleur!' I said. 'Fleur in the car behind! Her dad's driving – he wants us to pull over!'

'Well, I'm damned!' the coach driver said, but he found a lay-by, pulled over and Fleur – after profuse apologies from her dad to Mrs Mackie, the driver and everyone else – was allowed to come in.

After that the coach journey was boring.

We all fell asleep and only woke up when Erica shouted that we were coming into Dover.

We got off, the teachers herded us into groups and we queued and waited, then queued and waited some more, and after what seemed like hours we were trailed up the gangway, threatened with instant death if we so much as looked over the ship's rails, then put into the corner of a lounge with three teachers and given clipboards and a list of French menu words to practise. We did this for a while and then started making bored faces at each other. We were practically prisoners. Don't say the teachers were going to be looming over us all holiday . . .

'There's a disco downstairs!' Erica reported in a whisper, after disappearing for fifteen minutes – supposedly to the loo.

'Really?!' we whispered back.

'It's great!' she said. 'Make an excuse and come down.'

'Mrs Mackie!' I called immediately and urgently. 'Could I be excused, please!'

'And me!' called Fleur and several dozen others.

'Not all at once,' Mrs Mackie said, looking at us suspiciously.

'Oh, it's urgent! Terribly urgent!' Fleur said.

'I feel sick . . .' someone else whined piteously.

'I've really got to go now or I'll burst!'

In ones and twos we all got away. It was great; a proper disco with a light show, DJ and everything. Course, we all felt a bit daft at first, dancing about at that hour of the morning in salopettes and skiing jackets as well, but it was better than sitting upstairs with the teachers and yawning over French menu words. In the end practically the whole of the first-year girls – with the exception of goody-goody Alice – were there.

Every so often we'd go upstairs, sit still for five minutes or so, then innocently ask to be excused again.

'Upset stomach,' we'd remark piteously, or 'chill on the kidneys' – I remembered that one from Mum.

Mrs Mackie, I thought was rather vague and preoccupied for her, not noticing that at any given time three quarters of her class seemed to be in one very small loo.

When we got off the ship and on to the French coach, she counted us all up and then counted again and looked a bit worried.

'Could you go back to the ship again, Mickey,' she asked me, 'and check that no one's left in the disco.'

I was up and out of my seat before I realised what she'd said. I sat down again quickly. 'Disco? What disco?' I said innocently, but it was too late – Mrs Mackie was smiling from one side of her woolly hat to the other.

'The crafty old thing knew all the time,' Fleur whispered, and there were sheepish giggles all round.

The next coach journey was even longer, but because the countryside was French it wasn't so boring. We tried to work out what the big advertising signs said, ate our sandwiches, drank our fizzy drinks and got good and sticky.

This coach had a loo of its own, a tiny little sentry-box thing right in the middle, but no one wanted to use it – especially after the rumour went round that when you sat in it your head stuck out the top and a lighted sign came up at the front to say what you were doing. We all waited for what Mrs Mullins called 'comfort stops'.

By the time we got to our resort in the French Alps it was nearly midnight and we were all tired, hungry and fed up – especially when we saw that there was hardly any snow in the town. We'd thought we were going to walk straight into a Christmas card scene.

'There'll be plenty of snow higher up!'

18

Miss Hermitage said as she herded us into our hostel, but we felt too tired and irritable to believe her.

'She's got to say that,' Annabel muttered. 'I don't suppose they've seen as much as a flake all season.'

We stood around waiting to be assigned our rooms, too exhausted to speak to each other. I particularly hated everyone because Philippa had just remarked what a pity it was that my salopettes didn't match my anorak – had it come in a sale?

'Pull yourself together, girls!' Miss Hermitage said bracingly. 'A nice hot shower and bed, and you'll all feel wonderful in the morning.'

We made noises of disbelief, shuffling round in the dingy reception area of the hostel like waifs and strays.

Mrs Mackie and Mr Lloyd came back from the reception desk looking worried.

'I'm afraid there's some confusion over the rooms,' Mr Lloyd said, and we all stared at him, milling round in a great untidy circle.

'What do you mean?' Miss Lemming asked.

'They weren't expecting us until to-morrow,' he said uneasily. 'We haven't got anywhere to sleep tonight!'

Chapter Two
SATURDAY: SORTING OUT
THE STUCK-UPS

Cerise and Jasbir started crying, the rest of us just looked at each other in horror.

'There's been a change of staff here at the hostel,' Mr Lloyd said, shaking his head, 'and somehow, someone got the wrong end of the stick. They thought we were arriving midday tomorrow, instead of midnight tonight.'

'So what are we going to do?' Cerise wailed. 'Oo-oh, I don't like it here. I want to go home!'

'*I'll* want you to go home too, unless you stop that row at once!' Mrs Mackie said crisply. She put down her case. 'Now, as I see it, we've got two alternatives – we can get back on the coaches and make ourselves as comfortable as possible there for the night, or . . .'

'Mrs Mackie, they've just driven off!' Su shouted.

'Ah,' Mrs Mackie said, looking a bit put out – but only for a moment. 'Well, then,' she went on, 'the hostel manager says we can camp down here in the reception area for the night, so I suggest we do just that.'

'All of us?' I asked. There were about twenty-five of us first years and about twenty second and third years.

'The second and third years can have the lounge, and you lucky first years can have this lovely big reception area!' Mr Lloyd said, rubbing his hands together as if it was a treat.

'Oh, great . . .' we all moaned, and then started looking about for the best possible spaces: behind potted plants, next to a cupboard, under a bench, in an alcove.

A few staff who were on duty brought us some blankets, and after a few scuffles over ownership of hidey-holes we settled down – or tried to. I looked round: blankets, bodies and bags filled the reception area.

'Can't we have the lights off?' Philippa asked plaintively. 'I'll never be able to sleep otherwise.'

'Ooh no!' Cerise wailed. 'I'm afraid of the dark!'

'We can't have the lights out,' Mrs Mackie said from her vantage point of a chair, 'because not all the hostel guests are in yet.'

Just as she said that there came the squeal of car brakes from outside, followed by lots of door-slamming, and then about six girls – all a couple of years older than us, and all dressed up to the nines – came in giggling, screeching and calling to each other in loud voices.

Well, we all forgot about sleeping and sat up and looked at them – and they looked right back at us.

'Wherever have this little shower come from?' a tall, dark-haired girl said, looking down her nose at us. 'What an absolutely horrendous mess. Are they taking in people off the streets now?'

'Certainly looks like it,' a girl with red hair said. 'What *is* this place coming to?'

'If you don't mind,' Mrs Mackie said in an icy voice, 'some of us are trying to sleep.'

'How strange! One doesn't normally sleep in hotel doorways,' the first girl said.

'Take no notice, girls!' Mrs Mackie said. 'Settle down again, please.'

'Oh yes, do settle down again, girls!'

Carroty-hair echoed in an imitation of Mrs Mackie's voice.

We all looked at each other, not sure whether to giggle or look outraged.

'Really!' Mrs Mackie said, sitting upright and looking outraged for us. 'Don't you girls have a teacher in charge of you?'

'As a matter of fact, no,' Carroty-hair said. 'Though what it's got to do with you I can't imagine.'

'Nor can I!' another one said. 'If we want to bunk out on our last night it's entirely our own affair!'

'Dreadful,' Mrs Mackie muttered to herself. 'Absolutely no discipline. Take no notice, girls.'

The older girls started to move towards the stairs, all the time casting superior looks in our direction and making jokes which we couldn't quite hear.

'If it's you lot who're coming in our dorms,' a small fat girl wearing a lot of make-up said, 'well, just take care that you don't get put in number three – it's haunted!'

Cerise gave a scream.

'Ooh-no!' Jasbir wailed in fright.

'Don't be ridiculous!' Arina said sternly.

'Girls!' Mrs Mackie said. 'Take absolutely no notice whatsoever!' And as the last of the girls disappeared we all lay down again.

'Get them!' I whispered to Fleur – we were huddled in one of the prime spots, behind a bookcase.

'Stupid stuck-up lot,' she whispered back. 'I'm glad they're going tomorrow.'

'It's tomorrow now,' I said hoarsely, and nudged Fleur, but she'd fallen asleep.

I suppose we all slept a bit – not that it felt like it at six o'clock in the morning when the hostel staff started coming on duty and waking us up. We had a bit of a wash (those of us who could find our washbags in our suitcases, that is) and then we were led into the dining room to wait for breakfast.

We all sat round in the big room just looking at each other. No one was speaking – even Miss Hermitage had stopped saying bracing things. My eyes were all scratchy and I felt tired and miserable. As far as I could see, this most exciting holiday in the world – my first away from Mum and Dad, and the one where I was going to discover that I was an Olympic-class skier – looked like being an absolute disaster.

Something to eat came in: stale croissants and cups of coffee with skin on.

'Well, just what we need. Isn't this delicious?' said Miss Hermitage weakly – and then left hers.

The older girls came in, all looking tanned and super-fit. 'Oh, the bag people are up, then,' the fat one said, looking down her nose at us.

We looked back at them gloomily, not even bothering to try and get our own back. Another time and we would have set Alison on them – and if Araminta Eversage, our resident star, had been with us it would have been great – but the way we were feeling, no one could have cared less. We were all too tired and too fed up.

After breakfast, for apparently that was what the stale croissant was, we were allowed out to look around. It wasn't all that exciting. Now it was daylight we could see that the hostel was a huge, rather ugly building, its only claim to decoration being a statue on the forecourt of a tall gangly man, who turned out to be the one-time mayor. The road leading down from the hostel led into town, although we weren't allowed to go there – the excitement would have been too much for us – but by straining our eyes we could see a couple of lines of shops, bars and restaurants and loads and loads of hotels. At the back of the shops and all around us were the mountains, of course; some with chair lifts and some with small pulley lifts, and there was one huge set of cable cars in the distance. There was quite a bit of snow around, but it looked pretty sparse on the lower slopes.

When we went back inside there were a few rooms free, so some of us were allowed in to unpack. On the journey we'd promised our friends that we'd all stick together but, as Mrs Mackie had been vague about how many there were to a room, it had been difficult to plan anything definite. Now as the rooms became vacant she just read names off a clipboard and we went into them, too tired to object, just grateful that we didn't have to spend another night on the floor. Actually, it wasn't too bad; Fleur and I were together and we had Cerise, Annabel, Philippa, Mouse and Lorna in with us as well. We would have liked the twins and Su and Erica, but they were in another dorm – and they had awful Alison.

'You seven are in dormitory number three,' Mrs Mackie said to us, and there was a small shriek from Cerise which Mrs Mackie ignored. 'Go and unpack your things and have a shower.'

'Oh, but Mrs Mackie – that's the haunted room!' Cerise said. 'I can't possibly ... I couldn't ...'

'You can and you will!' Mrs Mackie said. 'Go!'

Cerise went; we all did. Our dorm was on the ground floor – most of the others were upstairs – and two of the Stuck-ups, as we called them, were still in there varnishing their nails.

'Quickly!' one said – it was the fat one with all the make-up. 'The great unwashed are coming in!'

'Lock up your valuables, everyone,' the other one said.

Fleur made a great show of dropping a curtsy as they went out, and I did the same.

'Good day, your highnesses,' I said.

'Thank you for being in the same room as us humble folk,' Fleur added, and all of us giggled – apart from Cerise.

'Is it true about the ghost?' she asked Fatty imploringly.

'Of course it is,' said Fatty in a superior voice. 'This room is totally haunted. We had a priest in, but even he couldn't get rid of it.'

'Oooh!' Cerise said in fright.

'Don't believe a word of it,' I said to Cerise. 'She's just trying to scare you.'

The girl looked at me darkly. 'Am I?' she said. 'Just you wait until the moon is full and the ghost walks . . .'

Cerise gave another scream, picked up her case and darted for the door. Annabel grabbed hold of her.

'What . . . what sort of ghost is it?' asked Cerise.

27

'The worst kind!' Fatty said in a sinister voice. 'A headless horseman!'

'I thought you said the ghost *walks*,' I said. 'If he's on a horse he couldn't, could he? Did you mean wait until the moon is full and the ghost *trots*?'

'You'll laugh on the other side of your face soon!' Fatty said darkly, going out.

Fleur and I looked at each other and she twisted her face into a gruesome contortion. 'I've often wondered what that means,' she said, 'how can you laugh on the other side of your face?'

'Search me!' I said.

'I don't know how you can laugh,' Cerise quavered. 'This is serious. I'm going to ring home; I shouldn't have to stay in a haunted room!'

'She was having you on!' I said.

'But I remember one of the older girls at school saying something about a ghost!'

'Oh, be quiet,' Fleur said, falling on to one of the beds, 'or the ghost round here will be you!'

'Or me if I don't get something to eat soon,' I added.

After unpacking we were allowed down to the town with a selection of teachers to pick up the boots, skis and poles that we'd hired. It took about forty tries before I found a pair of boots that felt even remotely comfortable,

and even then I wasn't at all sure that I'd
be able to move with such heavy great horrible things on the end of my legs. Still, I
reasoned to myself, everyone else managed
beautifully, so why should I be an exception? The trouble was, I usually was ...

Mrs Mullins allowed us into one of the
cafés and we spent practically half our
pocket money on cream cakes, apple strudels and hot chocolate, but at least we felt
a bit more human by the time we got back
to the hostel.

The Stuck-ups were in the reception area
checking out and, while we hung about
waiting for the rest of our class to come
back from the town, amused themselves
making rude comments about the fact that
we hadn't got boots and skis of our own, but
had had to hire them. Making lurid faces at
them every time Mrs Mullins wasn't looking
was about all we could think of doing to get
our own back – until I had a sudden idea. I
grabbed Fleur and Mouse and we went back
to our room. As well as Mouse being a fantastic painter, I happened to know that she
could also do pretty good lettering. And she
always had paints and paper with her ...

Fleur got some cardboard from the office,
we persuaded Cerise to give up some pink
hair-ribbon and we worked swiftly. By the
time the Stuck-ups' luxury coach pulled

away from the hostel (with them throwing their spare francs out of the windows for us) it had been provided with a beautiful sign tied to the back and saying, in both English and French (Fleur's mum was French so she could speak it pretty well):

HONK IF YOU THINK WE'RE STUCK UP AND STUPID!

As the coach drove through the town we were rewarded by the sound of honking horns. The first of many, we were sure . . .

Chapter Three
SUNDAY: A NEW SKI CHAMPION?

'Now, girls,' Miss Hermitage said, 'ski school won't start until tomorrow morning, but I thought I'd give you some of the basic movements today so that your new instructor doesn't find you completely green.'

'Ha ha! He'll find me green!' I said, pointing to my skiing outfit, but everyone just yawned at me.

We'd been told to go to bed at nine o'clock the previous night – *made* to, forced up the stairs groaning, moaning and complaining about how early it was every step of the way. We'd planned a midnight feast – when we'd been talking about it at home we'd said we were going to have one every single night – and someone had got a cassette player and tapes, and we'd written invitations to the other dorms, but though the crisps for the feast were bought and laid out on the bed, the invites were ready to be posted under doors and we'd sworn to stay awake until twelve, we were asleep by five past nine and that was the end of it.

I woke up at eight in the morning to six squashed packets of crisps – somehow I'd rolled on them in the night – and Mrs Mackie saying, 'Goodness me, how you all needed that sleep!'

'Now, hands up those girls who have been skiing before,' Miss Hermitage said, and most of the second and third-year girls – and Cerise, Annabel and Su from our lot – put their hands up and looked smug.

'Right, off you go with Mrs Mackie and Mr Lloyd,' Miss Hermitage said, 'and Miss Lemming and I will take the beginners to a nursery slope.'

'Nursery slope!' I said indignantly to Fleur. 'I don't fancy starting on a nursery slope. Why can't they call it something a bit more dignified?'

'What?' she asked, picking up her skis, poles and boots ready to set off.

I shrugged. 'Potential British ski champions slope or soon-to-be best skier in the world slope or something.'

'Perhaps you ought to see if you can stand up first,' she said over her shoulder. 'Hurry up!'

I picked up my skis, bent down for the poles and dropped one ski. The other swung sideways and hit Miss Lemming in the face.

'Sorry!' I said. I dropped both skis, picked up the poles and boots and made a grab for the skis again, but one slid away down the grassy slope.

'Really!' Miss Lemming said, going after it. 'It looks as if you're going to be a positive danger, Mickey – and you're not even on snow yet!'

'I'll be better on snow,' I puffed, picking up skis, poles and boots and dropping my gloves. 'It'll all come perfectly naturally to me on snow.' I bent for the runaway ski and stabbed myself in the foot with a pole.

'I think I'd better carry your skis,' Miss Lemming said. 'It might be safer.' She hoisted my skis, together with her own, on her shoulder, and we set off after the others.

'I take it that you've never ski'd before,' she said.

'Oh yes! I went to a dry ski slope with Annabel on her birthday.'

'How did you get on?'

'Couldn't even stand,' I said truthfully. 'I've just got this feeling that I'm going to be much better on snow, though. On snow I'm going to be absolutely brilliant!'

'I'm glad you're so confident,' Miss Lemming said, stepping smartly sideways to avoid being stabbed in the side by one of my swinging poles.

We followed Miss Hermitage and the others to the edge of a field just above the town; she'd managed to find one with a sprinkling of snow.

'We won't try and negotiate any of the ski pulleys today,' she said. 'Your ski instructor will help you with those when you can all do a few basic movements.'

'I'm dreading them!' Jasbir said to me as we formed a ragged line with Miss Hermitage in front of us. 'Some people never get the hang of them, apparently. They fall off every time and hold the whole queue up.'

'Oh – they're all right,' I said. 'They had them at the dry ski slope. Quite easy, really.'

'Did you use them, then?'

'Not exactly,' I said. 'I watched a lot, though. Piece of cake!'

'Mickey! Arina!' Miss Hermitage called.

34

'Are you ready to watch my demonstration of how to clip your boots on to your skis?'

'I'm Jasbir but I'm ready!' Jasbir called back.

Miss Hermitage sighed. 'I do wish you two hadn't had the same haircuts,' she said.

I quickly got out of my moon boots, into my ski boots and, almost breaking my fingers in the process, did up the clips. The boots felt awful – as if my feet were encased in a large side of beef.

'Now, place your skis at right angles to the slope . . .' Miss Hermitage called. 'Right angles, Mickey!'

'Right angles . . .' I muttered obediently, trying to cast my mind back to geometry lessons and wondering what she meant.

'That means not down the slope!' she yelled as, too late, both my skis slid gracefully away from me and away across the field.

Red-faced, I clomped off to get them back. By the time I'd climbed up to the top of the slope again, most of the others had their skis clipped on to their boots and were beaming, all pleased with themselves.

'Now, the rest of you stay there, remembering not to point down the slope,' Miss Hermitage said, 'while I help Mickey on to her skis.'

She showed me how to place the toe of my boot into the front of the ski binding and stamp down hard to lock it at the back, then said we were going to practise walking sideways up and down the slope until we felt comfortable on our skis.

I didn't exactly see how you could feel comfortable with feet a metre long, but I clambered up and down the slope with the others, poking people in the back with the tips of my skis, tripping them up with the backs and falling over every other minute. I'd managed a score of two teachers and four girls tripped and was thinking of starting a points system, when suddenly, almost at the top of the slope again, I found myself facing the wrong way – the down-slope way – and before I could right myself, started to sail away down the slope and across the field.

'Help!' I yelled. My arms flailed and I gathered speed, then I changed my mind about asking for help. I was actually doing it; I was skiing! 'I'm skiing!' I yelled. 'Look at me, everyone! Look how fast I'm going!'

'Drop your poles!' Miss Hermitage called. 'Concentrate on keeping your balance.'

'Look, I'm going really well!' I yelled. 'Take a photo, someone. Do I look . . .'

Do I look good, I'd been about to ask, but as I got faster I suddenly remembered that I didn't know how to stop, and just as I thought that, a tree stump appeared and I went into it and found out.

Miss Hermitage ski'd up. 'You do like to do things slightly differently to everyone else, don't you, Mickey?' she said.

I lay on the ground, winded. 'I've probably broken some bones,' I said weakly.

'You wouldn't get broken bones going at that slow speed,' Miss Hermitage said.

I looked at her indignantly. 'What d'you mean? I was going at least a hundred miles an hour.'

'Not quite,' she laughed, helping me to my feet.

We were exhausted by the time we got back to the hostel – not that we'd done much more than climb up and down the rotten slope about a million times and learn how to push off with our poles and do something which Miss Hermitage called 'snow ploughs'. Apparently once you could do these properly they helped to slow you down and, if you didn't get the front of your skis locked together so you fell over into a heap, helped you stop gracefully. At the moment, mine kept locking, but I was sure I'd be all right on proper snow. Just put me on proper thick snow and I'd be perfectly all right . . .

On the way back to the hostel we made up our midnight feast stockpile with more crisps, some dry biscuits and butter, chocolate, fizzy drinks and apple pies. We also bought postcards to write home. I wrote to Mum and Dad telling them I'd been on a black run already, but not to worry because I was a natural, and Cerise made us all sign a card to Jane. It said:

> *Dear Araminta,*
> *We really miss you. There are some gorgeous tanned ski instructors here and you would really enjoy yourself. When you do the next* Village Life *episode could you wave to me?*
> *Love from your best friend Cerise and all the others.*

After we'd written our cards we had a little pick at the midnight feast, which we'd hidden under Fleur's bed, while we waited to have baths. Baths and washes were a bit tricky because there was only one bathroom between each dorm and, if you didn't get in there sharpish, you didn't get any hot water. Cerise got into ours first, taking pink bath oil, strawberry face pack and half the Body Shop, and seemed set to spend the rest of the night in there.

'What *is* she doing?' Philippa asked crossly – she'd bagged the next bath. 'I can't believe that anyone could be so long.'

'Well, she's got her pre-bath lotion, in-bath lotion and after-bath lotion,' I said, 'not to mention strawberry-flavoured hair mousse.'

Fleur gave a sudden scream. 'Hair mousse! I saw it on the side and thought it was something to eat. I had a little dip into it with a biscuit!'

'Don't be so ridiculous,' Philippa said, while Fleur nodded to me that she *had*, she really had. Philippa walked up and down tutting and, just to pass the time, we had a fizzy drink each.

'I know how to get her out,' Fleur said suddenly.

'What?' I asked. 'Pretend Jane's arrived?'

'No. Pretend the ghost has! Someone could make some scratching noises outside the bathroom door,' she went on, 'and then someone else could do some faint moaning.'

'And rattling of chains!' I said excitedly. 'And coconut shells clapping together for horses' hooves and the thudding of bodies being dragged along the ground and . . .'

'I think that might be going a bit too far,' Mouse interrupted. 'Just the scratching and the moaning would be fine.'

We thought it appropriate that Mouse should do the mousely scratching and Fleur and I, after having a bit of a row about who could do a ghostly moan best, were elected to moan in turns. I was to moan softly and pathetically, Fleur was to moan more eerily and frighteningly. We had a practice – first eating an apple pie each because we were starving – then went out into the corridor and down to the bathroom.

Cerise was humming the theme tune from *Village Life* and didn't hear Mouse's scratching until Mouse had turned it into a loud scrape. Once she'd heard it she stopped humming.

'Who's there?' she called. Mouse scratched some more.

I nudged Fleur to do a moan and she nudged me back.

'Soft and pathetic moan first,' she whispered.

I nodded and did a sad and sorry little moan. 'Who is it?' Cerise called. 'Is it someone who wants to come in?'

'Whoo-ooo!' Fleur moaned eerily. 'Whoo-ooo!'

'Who is it? What's that?' Cerise asked in a frightened voice.

I put my mouth right to the keyhole for a whispery and wistful moan. There was a scuffle behind me and someone poked me in the ribs.

'Quiet!' I said. 'Don't do any more scratching now. This is going to be a really sad and pitiful moan.' I giggled. 'The sort of moan Mrs Mackie gives us when she's talking about how wonderful her last lot of first years were and . . .'

I felt a hand on my shoulder. 'What are you doing down there, Michelle?' Mrs Mackie asked.

I shot upright. 'Just . . . er . . . seeing if Cerise has finished in the bathroom yet.'

'Might I suggest you ask her, then,' Mrs Mackie said. 'And what was all that about moaning?'

I rubbed my legs. 'Oh . . . er . . . I was just moaning to myself about how stiff I am. After skiing, you know . . .'

'I see,' she said, giving me the steely eye treatment.

I smiled at her glassily. 'See you at dinner, Mrs Mackie!' I said, shooting off down the corridor back to our dorm.

'You rotten lot!' I said to Mouse and Fleur, who were rolling round the dorm laughing. 'Why didn't you tell me she'd come along!'

'We tried to – Mouse poked you – but you wouldn't take any notice,' Fleur said.

Cerise appeared, pink-faced and matching her bath towel.

'Who was that outside the door?' she asked. 'There was a lot of funny noises

41

and groaning and then I heard Mrs Mackie talking to someone.'

'Dunno,' we all said, helping ourselves to dry biscuits. 'Didn't hear a thing.'

'It was really strange,' Cerise said fearfully. 'They were really weird and ghostly sorts of noises.'

Philippa got all her stuff together to go for her bath. 'Perhaps it *was* the ghost,' she said, 'and Mrs Mackie saw it off. She wouldn't stand for any ghosts, would she?'

'It certainly sounded very funny ...' Cerise said.

'I shouldn't stay in the bathroom too long again, then,' Fleur said, 'just in case.'

Annabel, trying to hide a smile, made for the door. 'Shall I tell the others that the midnight feast is definitely on for tonight?' she asked.

Everyone nodded. 'What have we got to eat?' I asked.

Fleur looked under her bed, then she pulled out empty crisp packets, empty fruit pie boxes, empty drinks cans and empty biscuit wrappers.

'There doesn't appear to be a lot left,' she said, then added, 'Oh yes, there's some butter — but it was left next to the radiator so it's in a puddle.'

We all looked at each other.

'Better cancel the midnight feast,' I said.

Chapter Four

MONDAY: A GNOME, A GHOST AND A FOOD STRIKE

Clutching all our bits, and panting and struggling under half a ski shop of clothing, a group of us struggled out of the hostel and towards the bus that was to take us towards the ski lifts and our first proper skiing lesson.

'I don't know why I bothered to try and lose weight,' Fleur said, puffing and red in the face. 'Whatever you wear when you're skiing you look huge. I feel ... like a bloat fish.'

'What's a bloat fish?' Annabel wanted to know.

Fleur shrugged. 'Dunno. It just sounds enormously fat.'

I tried to move my arms and legs under what felt like ten jumpers and a layer of foam rubber. 'In that case I feel like two bloat fish,' I said. 'I'm wearing practically everything I brought with me. I can hardly move.'

'It's because you've got a heavy anorak and not a real skiing jacket,' Cerise said knowledgeably. 'Real skiing jackets are very warm without being thick.'

'This *is* a real skiing jacket,' I said, annoyed. 'It's an alpine-weight one, especially for mountaineers.'

'Oh yes?' She didn't believe me, but she suddenly thought of something else and gave a little Cerise-type squeal. 'Ooh! I've forgotten my protective make-up! When we get on the top of the mountain my skin will absolutely shrivel.'

'But you put about half a ton of stuff on your face this morning,' Philippa said. 'I saw you.'

'Yes, but Mummy bought me some special fluorescent stick make-up,' Cerise said. 'You wipe it across your nose and cheekbones in stripes and it protects vulnerable areas.'

'Well, you can't go back now,' I said, 'Mrs Mackie will go mad – our dorm was last out as it was.'

'You'll have to protect vulnerable areas

44

tomorrow,' Fleur said, pulling at a cerise-coloured arm.

'It'll be too late by then,' Cerise said worriedly, but allowed Fleur to hurry her on.

We reached the bus and, once we'd stowed our skis in the special carrier on the back and heaved ourselves aboard, I mentally checked to see that I'd remembered everything; I didn't want everyone groaning at me and saying, *'Typical!'* if I got to the top and found I'd forgotten something vital. I had it all, though: boots, poles, skis, gloves, hat, goggles, bum bag with money, tissues and lip stuff.

The bus drove for ten minutes or so towards the ski-lift stations. Here several huge cable cars were going up and down the mountain range and here also what seemed like the entire population of the town plus their aunties were crowding to get on. Once at the top we were going to be divided up into our ski classes for the week and then go off with our ski instructor for lessons. I was going to be good. I *was*. Once I was with a real ski instructor on real snow I'd be great . . .

Mr Lloyd had charge of about ten of us to see that we all got in the same cable car and didn't get lost along the way. It took about fifteen minutes to get to the front of one of the queues, but eventually, packed like sardines – or bloat fish, probably – we were in a cable car. It gave a lurch, took off and suddenly soared above the town while we stared out of the window making admiring noises at the fantastic view. Halfway up the mountain we could see for miles: the town spread out beneath us, some little cars going along the road, our hostel with the mayor's statue outside, the crowd immediately below us still waiting for their cable cars, the little pile of skis . . . I gave a sudden scream.

'What is it, Mickey?' Mr Lloyd asked. 'Not frightened of heights, are you?'

I looked at Mr Lloyd and smiled a sickly smile. 'No, I've . . . er . . . forgotten my skis,' I said. 'I just rested them on the wall downstairs while we were queuing and then I forgot all about them.'

'Typical!' Philippa said, and I glowered at her.

Mr Lloyd looked at me and shook his head wearily. 'Oh dear, oh dear,' he said. 'Well, we'll get up to the top, I'll hand everyone else over to one of the other teachers and then you and I will go down again.'

'You don't have to come. I can go on my own,' I said with dignity.

'I'm sure you can,' he said, giving me a piercing look, 'but the idea is not exactly a comforting one. You'll probably end up skiing in Andorra.'

Half an hour later we were back on the top of the mountain again. There were still crowds trying to get into the cable cars but we'd managed to squash ourselves in with Miss Hermitage's group of girls.

At the upper cable-car station, as far up the mountain as you could go, there was a huge expanse of thick but very walked-upon snow, small lifts going off into different directions, a restaurant and a coffee-bar-type place with people sitting outside sunbathing or reading. I stomped around in my two pairs of thick socks and my moon boots – also a sale bargain and a size too big – and found Fleur and the others.

'What did Mr Lloyd say to Miss Hermitage?' Philippa asked me as soon as I got to them. 'I saw them squashed together in the lift.'

I shrugged. 'Good morning, I think,' I said, wondering whether to put on my hat and gloves to save carrying them.

'Is that all?' she said, frowning. 'He must have said more than that.'

I shook my head. 'He didn't have much chance – all the second-year girls kept asking him things.'

'Well, did he say it in a meaningful way?' she demanded.

'Why should he say good morning in a meaningful way?' Fleur wanted to know.

Philippa gave her craftiest smile. 'Because I think he fancies her. I think there's Something Going On,' she announced.

Cerise clapped her fluffy cerise hands. 'Ooh!' she said. 'In love! How romantic!'

'How d'you work that out?' I asked.

'I've been watching them,' Philippa said. 'He sat next to her on the coach over here – practically knocked Miss Lemming down to get to her – and every time we see Miss Hermitage he's somewhere around carrying her skis or her bag.'

'Or looking deeply into her eyes!' Cerise said eagerly. 'He was definitely looking deeply into her eyes at breakfast.'

'That doesn't mean anything's going on,' Annabel said. 'Perhaps she had a smut in her eye and he was looking for it.'

'Bet it does!' Philippa said. 'I've got a nose for these things. Remember it was me who told you all what was in the poison cupboard! I'm nearly always right!'

'Oh yes? What about Mrs Potter being arrested?' Fleur said, just as Cerise interrupted to ask if there *was* something going on, did we think Miss Hermitage might choose her to be a bridesmaid?

48

Before we could argue with Philippa any more, though, or jump on Cerise, Miss Hermitage was putting us into groups and Cerise and Annabel and some of the other intermediate skiers were led off to a tall, very blond and very bronzed ski instructor who looked as if he ought to be in a pop group.

'Look at Cerise's face!' Fleur said, nudging me, and I looked over to see Cerise, her face as pink as her ski suit, gazing at her ski instructor with glazed, hero-worshipping eyes.

Our ski instructor didn't look like a pop star. He was short, dumpy and had a red woolly hat with a bell on the end. We christened him Gnome.

Gnome spoke to us about skiing generally, and told us that we must obey strictly 'Ze rules of ze mountains'. We put on our skis (it took me ages to bend through the layers of clothes) and jumped up and down to get the feel of them, then lastly did some warm-up exercises, flailing our arms round and around like windmills. I had Alison flailing next to me and she managed to hit me in the face twice – and not by accident, either, because both times she smiled her nasty smile when she did it.

Once we were warmed up we followed Gnome – by concentrating hard I stayed upright – to a quietish spot with a small slope covered with snow. He said he wanted to see what we could do.

'We try ze snow plough first,' he said encouragingly, and pushed off and did perfect snow plough turns for us to copy, zig-zagging left and right, all the way down to the bottom of the slope. One by one the rest of us – about ten in all – pushed off and slowly, gingerly, edged our way down. I reached the bottom without falling!

'I knew I could do it on real snow and with a real instructor,' I said to Fleur excitedly. 'Did you watch me? Did I look good?'

'Sort of,' she said cautiously.

'Go on! I bet I looked like I was in the Winter Olympics, didn't I? Real stylish.'

'Well, you were sort of hunched up with your bottom sticking out – you looked more ·like a baboon trying to drive a car,' she said, and I gave her a push which sent her slightly sideways and into Lorna, who flailed around a bit and then slid swiftly to the bottom of the slope without stopping, squealing all the way.

'*Veery* good, all of you!' Gnome lied when we'd all snow-ploughed down and were standing in a straggly line again. 'But remember to bend ze knees at all times. We must bend ze knees!'

We heard quite a lot about knees throughout the morning because Gnome kept shouting about them. Especially to me. He also shouted things like: 'Keep ze seat in!' 'Keep ze back straight!' or, quite often, 'Oh no, Mickeee!'

By lunchtime I was as tired as if I'd climbed right the way up the rotten mountain on my hands and knees. I hadn't fallen over too many times, though.

We broke for lunch, left Gnome and made our way to the restaurant where we queued for spaghetti bolognaise, swopped notes with everyone else and insisted that we were totally, absolutely exhausted and could never walk another step again. The teachers – Mr Lloyd was sitting next to Miss Hermitage, Philippa gleefully pointed out – were sitting on a table together at the end, laughing and joking together and for all the world looking hardly like teachers at all, more like normal people.

We girls sat down together on one of the long wooden tables.

'Food!' Fleur said, looking at her spaghetti as if it was a casket of gold. 'Real food!'

'What we get to eat at the hostel is absolutely disgusting,' Arina said. 'I've never seen anything like it. French food is usually gorgeous.'

51

'I've never been abroad but even our school dinners are better than what we have here,' I said. I shuddered. 'What about that pork chop yesterday!'

'There was no pork on it,' Fleur said. 'It was a fat chop.'

'And that red cabbage!' Lorna said.

'And those greasy chips!'

'Chip!' Philippa corrected. 'I only got one.'

'Perhaps we ought to go on strike!' I said. 'If we all refuse to eat the food then they'll have to do something about it.'

Everyone agreed it was a great idea, and because we were having lunch we didn't feel it would be too hard. Even so, Fleur was despatched to the coffee bar to buy up chocolate, biscuits and jelly beans for the midnight feast our dorm was definitely, without a shadow of a doubt, having that night.

Cerise appeared just as we were leaving for our afternoon skiing lessons.

'Where have you been?' I asked. 'You haven't got time to eat now.'

'Eat?' she said, looking at us dreamily. 'How could I eat?'

'Quite easily,' Fleur said, 'what you do is put something in your mouth and then move your jaws up and down.'

'I don't want to eat,' she said, sighing. 'I

couldn't. I feel positively off my food now that I've met Jean-Paul. I shall probably never eat again.'

Fleur giggled. 'There! We knew it, didn't we, Mickey?'

'Well, you wouldn't be able to eat either, if you had him for your instructor,' Cerise said with another sigh. 'He's gorgeous. He's got the most beautiful green eyes and long legs and . . .'

'We've seen him,' I said.

'What's yours like?' Cerise asked.

'Well, he's shaped like a rugby ball and looks like Noddy,' Fleur said.

In the afternoon there were two more hours of bending ze knees, gradually going further and further down the slope and doing giant 'V' steps up again, digging the edges of our skis into the snow so that we wouldn't slide down. Or not often. The next day, Gnome promised that he'd take us up on one of the pulley lifts to another, more exciting slope.

When we got back to the hostel there were several fights over the bathroom, although Cerise was in and out in a flash because, as well as being frightened that the ghost would come, she said she was in a hurry to write to Araminta to tell her about her wonderful skiing instructor.

Talking about the ghost gave us a good

idea, so we wrote some midnight-feast invitations out in a shaking, ghostly hand.

*COME TO ROOM 3, THE ONLY
HAUNTED DORM FOR A FEAST
UPON THE HOUR OF MIDNIGHT!
BRING FOOD AND PLEASE DRESS
TO MATCH THE SPIRIT (ha ha) OF
THE OCCASION.*

We posted them under the doors of those
we wanted to come, leaving out Alison
because she'd not only flailed at me but
also pushed Mouse into a snowdrift and
dropped someone's gloves into a ravine,
and then we went downstairs to eat. Or
not eat.

Dinner was a yellow lettuce leaf, a piece
of cucumber, half a tomato and something
pink and spongy which was a mystery to
most of us but which Su (who knew all
about food because her mum and dad owned
a Takeaway) swore was tongue.

Well, even if I hadn't been on strike I
couldn't have eaten tongue so we first-
years all pushed our plates to one side
and steadfastly refused to touch a thing,
all except for Alice, who couldn't do anything so naughty as go on a food strike
and Wendy, who said she was sorry but

she was so hungry she could eat a horse. (Fleur told her darkly that she probably was.)

In the end, though, and much to our fury, our strike didn't make any difference, because the waitresses were so used to us leaving the food that they thought it was a day like any other and cleared our full plates away without seeming to notice anything was up. We tried to find out how to say 'food strike' in French so we could look them in the eye accusingly and say it, but no one seemed to know.

After dinner it was card games and fun (well, that's what they said it was) with the teachers and at about eleven, exhausted after traipsing up and down mountains, we were quite pleased to be sent off to bed. We got the midnight feast all sorted, Annabel set her alarm watch for midnight and we went straight to sleep. We planned to whip the sheets off our beds and dress up as ghosts as soon as Annabel woke us.

I must have fallen asleep straight away, because it seemed like only minutes later that Annabel was shaking me.

'Wake up!' she said. 'It's midnight and I can't get anyone else to budge. They're all sleeping like logs.'

'I want to sleep like a log, too,' I muttered, and I put my head under the pillow and went straight off again.

It was no good, the ghostly midnight feast would have to be the next night . . .

Chapter Five
TUESDAY: CERISE AND
MR SUPERCOOL

'Now,' Gnome said, 'eet is quite simple. All you do is stand with your partner and, when the pulley comes round, take it and place it behind ze bottom, then lean back and let ze workings to pull you up ze mountain.'

'There!' I said to Jasbir. 'I told you it was easy.'

Our skiing class shuffled forwards in the long line of people waiting to go up the mountain on the pulley lift. 'You must remember,' Gnome said warningly, 'don't seet on ze pulley. We rest only on him.'

We watched as yet another pair of skiers sped smoothly upwards. 'Looks all right,' I said to Fleur. 'Coming on with me?'

'If you like,' she said, 'but don't wobble, will you? Did you hear what Gnome said? Once you get on you've got to stay perfectly still and point your skis forward.'

'I know!' I said, and then gasped in amazement as Cerise and her class – headed by Mr Supercool – went by on their way down the mountain.

'Did you see Cerise's face?' I yelped.

Fleur nodded. 'Like a Red Indian's! Pink fluorescent stripes on her cheekbones . . .'

'And luminous white lips!'

'It's that special make-up of hers. She said that the Royals wear it for skiing,' Jasbir said. 'She thinks that her ski instructor –'

'Mr Supercool?'

'Yes, him – she thinks that once he sees her wearing all that trendy skiing make-up he's going to fall madly in love with her.'

Behind us, Arina and Lorna giggled.

'Hurry up, you lot!' came a call from further back down the queue. 'You're holding the line up!'

Fleur and I shuffled forward, had our new lift passes which hung round our necks stamped, and went through the wooden barrier to stand on the platform where the T-bars swung round to take us up.

Gnome stood beside us to give words of encouragement.

'Put ze poles and gloves in one hand, keep ze other hand free to hold on to ze pulley!' he said. 'Here he comes!'

The pulley clanged into place behind us, Fleur grabbed it, pushed it behind us, then we both grabbed for the central T-bar, leaned back slightly to be ready and, as the pulley moved up, we both fell off!

'You took up all the room!' Fleur said accusingly as we tried to pick ourselves up from the muddy snow.

'I did not!' I said heatedly. 'You were sitting on it sideways.'

'I was not! You know you're no good at these sort of – '

'Quickly! Aah, too late!' Gnome said, as I got up – only to get pushed sideways by the next T-bar coming through.

'Hold tighter next time,' Fleur commanded. 'And don't take up all the room.'

'Don't sit on it all wonky, then!'

'Here he comes!' Gnome said, and this time we managed to grab hold of the T-bar successfully and get pulled up the slope a little way – but then somehow Fleur's skis got tangled up in mine and we both ended up flat on our faces in the snow again.

'Oh dear,' Gnome said, as more empty T-bars went up without us. 'Sometimes we have zis. Sometimes ze girls do not seem to get ze message.'

'I get the message!' Fleur said, glowering at me. 'It's her! She's doing it all wrong.'

I glowered back, really hurt. This was my best friend speaking!

'You go now wiz a twin,' Gnome said to Fleur – he'd given up trying to tell them apart. 'Mickey will try wiz ze ozzer twin.'

I stood to one side while – much to my fury – Fleur and Arina got on the T-bar and moved slowly and smoothly up the mountain.

'I told you it was you!' Fleur called over her shoulder as she went into the distance.

'Now we try again!' Gnome said, settling me and Jasbir into place. 'Remember not to seet on the T-bar. And point zee skis straight ahead.'

Nervously I stood, teeth gritted, and waited until the T-bar came round. Just as Gnome grabbed it and put it into position Jasbir said, 'I wanted to go with Arina. I know I shall fall off with you!' and promptly did, pulling me with her.

The next time we tried I dropped both my gloves just at the wrong moment, bent down to pick them up and got whacked on the bottom by the T-bar coming round behind me. By this time the queue behind us was building up, and because everyone queued alongside the bit where you got on

– or tried to get on – my efforts became an amusing cabaret for half of Park Wood and anyone else who wanted a laugh.

After another couple of goes I was hot, horribly embarrassed and scarlet in the face. Things were made worse when, much to my disgust, Jasbir managed to get on the T-bar successfully with Mouse. I tried again with Philippa but in the end I had to go with Gnome; he put his arm round me and by sheer force held me on to the T-bar so I couldn't wobble and fall off.

'Eet is nothing; not to worry,' he said on the way up. 'For some eet comes easy. For others . . . not so easy. We go on a single lift tomorrow. You find it better.'

'Oh yeah?' I muttered, hating pulley lifts, hating skiing and hating everyone who'd managed to get up without falling off.

'At last! It's almost time to go back,' Fleur said when Gnome and I eventually arrived at the top, and I was all ready to especially hate her when she laughed and said she was only kidding. She said she and Arina hadn't known how to get off when they'd got to the top so the T-bar had dragged them both along over some gravel, and they'd had visions of being swung down the slope again, but at the last minute they'd managed to fling themselves off and into a puddle. I smiled in a wobbly way;

61

under the influence of Gnome, I'd sailed off the T-bar beautifully, so at least I'd done something right.

Up where we were supposed to be at last, we snow-ploughed slowly all over the place without, luckily for me, having to go on another lift. At lunchtime we were back to where we'd started – at the top cable-car station. We took off our skis, plunged them into the snow with everyone else's (mine kept falling over), changed into our moon boots and were just going into the restaurant for food when Philippa beckoned us all together and whispered that Mr Lloyd and Miss Hermitage were sitting together in the corner on their own and she was absolutely and positively sure that they were holding hands. Fleur and I were delegated to go and look and make sure.

'What'll we say?' I whispered as we made our way across the restaurant.

'Make it up when we get there,' Fleur said out of the corner of her mouth. 'Improvise!'

The happy couple were deep in conversation and didn't even look up as we approached.

I coughed loudly. 'Good morning's skiing, Miss Hermitage?' I asked politely.

Miss Hermitage glanced up. 'Yes, thank

you, Mickey,' she said, cool as anything.
'Why do you ask?'

'Just being polite,' I said, craning to
look over the wooden table and see their
hands.

'Good day's skiing, Mr Lloyd?' Fleur
asked, equally politely.

'Super, thank you!' Mr Lloyd said, and
then they both stared hard at us, waiting
for us to go away.

'Do you find your gloves very useful?' I
suddenly asked in a fairly desperate bit of
improvisation.

'Gloves?' they asked in puzzled voices.

'Yes . . . gloves. Mine . . . er . . . don't
seem very warm,' I went on doggedly.

'Nor do mine!' Fleur said, catching on.
'My hands are always cold. My fingers are
quite chapped.'

'Mine, too!' I said, pretending to examine
my hands worriedly. 'What are yours like,
Miss Hermitage?'

'My hands are lovely and warm, thank
you,' she said. 'Not a chap in sight!'

'Yours all right?' Fleur asked Mr Lloyd.

'Absolutely fine,' he said. 'And fascinat-
ing though this discussion is, I do believe
your friends are waiting for you. That's
them over at the other side of the restaurant giggling hysterically, isn't it?'

'Probably,' Fleur said in a careless voice,

and we backed off and went to give our reports.

'Well?' Philippa demanded.

Fleur and I nodded excitedly. We weren't absolutely sure they'd been holding hands, but they easily could have been and we wanted to keep things going.

'I hope it's not just a holiday romance,' Cerise said worriedly, to the accompaniment of our groans. 'I hope he's not going to string her along and then break her heart ...' She gazed out into the snow. 'It happens all the time,' she added mournfully.

In the afternoon Gnome found us another snowy slope with a bump in the middle of it (he called it a 'mogul') where I fell every single time I tried to ski over it.

I had to face it; I didn't seem all that wonderful at skiing. Some of the others were picking it up quickly, doing little jumps and getting cries of 'Super!' from Gnome, but all I got was cries of 'Sacre bleu!' Even horrible Alison had turned out to be quite good and amused herself by saying to me in a withering voice, 'Aren't you useless,' 'How pathetic!' and other sarcastic things.

We were determined, whatever happened, to have a midnight feast that night, so much to the teachers' surprise (and after a dinner of macaroni cheese without any cheese, tasting of cotton wool) we said we'd like an early night.

'But it's only nine o'clock,' said Mrs Mackie in surprise. 'Are you sure? We were thinking of going on a sleigh ride.'

I did a huge and false yawn. 'We're all really tired ... it's the fresh air,' I said. 'Couldn't we go on the sleigh ride another night?'

'I suppose so,' Mrs Mackie said. She raised her eyebrows. 'An early night ... how unusual.'

The idea, of course, was to have a few hours' sleep and then be awake all bright and cheerful at midnight, but when we got up to our dorm and laid down and tried to sleep, no one could. We wrote some postcards home and Cerise wrote to Jane again.

'I've asked her advice about Jean-Paul,' she said – that was Mr Supercool's real name. 'Araminta's experienced in these sort of things. She'll know what to do.'

'We go home Saturday. You won't get a reply by then!' Mouse said.

'I might,' Cerise said. 'If she knows it's urgent she might send a telegram.'

We all laughed and Cerise said we were being cruel and didn't know what it was like to be really in love with someone who

65

was out of reach. She clasped her hands together. 'It's just like in *Village Life* where the girl who's dying is in love with the vet,' she said wistfully.

Philippa grabbed her letter.

Dear Araminta, she read out in Cerise's simpering voice, *I'm sure Jean-Paul likes me because he selected me to do parallel turns and when I asked him if he had a girlfriend he smiled in a meaningful way and said 'not at the moment'. Should I come right out and tell him I like him or shall I send him a letter? Write back quickly and tell me ...*

'Give it back! You're being horrible!' Cerise said, making a grab for the letter and only succeeding in tearing it.

Everyone told Philippa to give it back so she did, whereupon Cerise took it to bed with her, wrote some more and then fell asleep. The rest of stayed awake gossiping and, about eleven-thirty, got our sheets off the beds and draped them round us, ghost-style, ready for the feast. I thought we ought to tear two eye-holes in them to see through but Lorna said we mustn't, and then Fleur had the brilliant idea of putting Cerise's luminous white lipstick all over our faces.

We looked fantastically ghosty when we'd finished, and Philippa had a practise flutter up and down the corridors and swore that she'd met an old lady who'd fainted clean away at the sight of her.

Just before midnight Fleur and I decided to go and wake the others, and flitted down the corridor to the dorm where the twins, Su and Erica were.

They hadn't gone to sleep, either, and were already dressed up in their sheets. Erica had hers right over her head and had also painted a balloon with a face, which she had under her arm.

They pointed towards Alison's bed and made a face.

'She knows something's up,' Erica whispered, 'so we've all put pillows in our beds. If she wakes she'll think we're still there.' Making quite a lot of ghosty noises along the way, we went back to our dorm. I woke Cerise, forgetting she hadn't seen us put on the white make-up, and she let out a terrible scream.

'No! Help!' she yelled. 'Save me from the ghost, someone!'

'It's all right, it's me – Mickey!' I said.

'Oh oh . . .' whimpered Cerise. 'You looked so awful, glowing in the dark. I thought the ghost had come for me.'

'We're wearing your white lipstick all over our faces,' I explained, 'but be quiet or you'll wake the teachers.'

'Some of the teachers are awake,' said

Philippa. 'I've just been doing a spot of investigating and there's a light on in Mr Lloyd's room!'

Cerise stopped being terrified and sat up. 'And is Miss Hermitage in there?'

'That's what we're going to find out,' Philippa said.

We ate the midnight feast, which didn't take long, and then we flitted around the corridors a bit, woo-hooing in a ghosty way, hoping to find people to scare but not seeing anyone.

'Time to investigate Mr Lloyd and Miss Hermitage,' Philippa announced and so, flapping our sheets, we made our way to Mr Lloyd's room. I'm not sure what we were going to do when we got there — try and see through the keyhole, perhaps, but as we stood there nudging each other and giggling, the door suddenly opened and Mrs Mackie stood there, holding a glass of something. We all gawped at her. We weren't expecting to find Mrs Mackie in Mr Lloyd's room!

'My goodness me!' she said, startled. 'I thought I heard a noise. Whatever are you all doing?'

Cerise started giggling (she looked weirder than anyone because she'd put fluorescent pink all over her face), Philippa gave a nervous cackle and Erica's 'head' squeezed out from under her arm and bounced on to the floor.

'Come along!' Mrs Mackie said briskly. 'What are you all up to?'

'We've just . . . er . . . been having a little get-together to er . . . discuss French verbs!' I said – I was getting good at improvising. 'We didn't think you'd mind.'

'Dressed like that?' she asked disbelievingly.

'And we came along to see if you'd join us!' Erica said.

'Well!' Mrs Mackie said, and she suddenly laughed and pushed the door a little wider. 'Why don't you join us, instead?'

We stared. All the teachers were there – including nasty strict Mrs Taylor.

'We'd better not, thanks all the same,' Fleur said, backing off. She yawned falsely. 'About time we got some sleep.'

Mr Lloyd spoke up. 'Oh, we insist, don't we, ladies!' he said in a jovial voice, waving his glass.

So we went in and had to sit down and have a glass of orange. We explained that we were dressed up as ghosts because the girls who'd had our dorm last had told us it was haunted.

'It is, too!' Cerise said earnestly. 'And the ghost travels to the bathroom. I was in there a couple of nights ago and there were shocking cries from outside.' She gave a dramatic shudder. 'It sounded like were-wolves – werewolves shrieking unearthly shrieks that went on for hours and hours!' she exaggerated.

'I didn't realise we sounded that good,' Fleur whispered.

Mrs Mackie went to get us some crisps and after we'd eaten these and polished off another glass of orange, we stood up ready to go.

'We'd better be off,' Erica said, nudging Cerise hard to stop her talking.

'Thank you for the orange and crisps,' we all said, and the teachers waved their glasses at us and, looking uncannily human, wished us all a good day's skiing the next day.

The twins and Erica went back to their own dorm and we, yawning widely, went back to ours. Something really weird had happened, though: all our beds had been swung around to point the wrong way and, written in a shaky hand on the mirror in the tiny bit of Cerise's white lipstick which had been left, was:

Dorm 3 ghost haunts again!

Well, talk about spooky.

Chapter Six
WEDNESDAY: MISSION IMPOSSIBLE!

'Who d'you think it was, then?' Su asked during the meal laughingly known as breakfast.

'Must have been someone from another dorm,' I said. 'One of the second-years, perhaps.'

'Or maybe it was someone who works here,' Erica said. 'Perhaps they always play tricks – that's why those girls who stayed here last week said there was a ghost.'

We looked at the dour waitresses serving our hard rolls and hot-chocolate-with-skin-on, then looked at each other and shook our heads.

'Can't be them,' I said, 'none of them

look as if they know what a joke is. And the manageress wouldn't bother – she's too busy trying to think of new and even more revolting meals.'

'Maybe it was Alison,' Fleur whispered, gnawing at a hard roll. 'Perhaps she was only pretending to be asleep and, when we went into Mr Lloyd's room, she crept in.'

I shook my head. 'It doesn't seem like her sort of thing, somehow. She's more into kicking people under the table and screwing up homework.'

'I don't know why you're all wondering about it!' Cerise suddenly burst out. 'The message said it was the ghost and that's who it was!'

'Ghost?' Mrs Mullins said, coming round distributing our lift passes. 'What's all this about a ghost?'

Cerise blurted out about the message on the mirror before anyone could stop her. 'The others think it was someone playing a trick but I know it's the ghost!' she finished. 'I've heard it, you see. I told you – it came outside the bathroom and wailed at me!'

Mrs Mullins lifted her eyebrows. 'Well, perhaps you're right. We've been staying here for years and I've heard talk of a ghost before. Apparently it takes someone who's psychic to set it off.'

'That's me!' Cerise squealed. 'I'm ...

whatever-you-said. Mummy always says I'm . . . that word!'

'I'm sure you are,' Mrs Mullins said, going off smiling to herself.

'Let's have another midnight feast tonight to see if anything else happens!' Erica said excitedly. 'You lot can come in our dorm this time.'

'What about Alison, though?' Jasbir asked, pulling a face. 'I don't want her to be there. Yesterday she pulled my ski pass round my neck so tightly that I was nearly strangled.'

'You just want to give her a hefty shove!' Arina said. 'You're too soft, you are. She's only got to look at you and you burst out crying.'

'I do not!' Jasbir said heatedly.

'You do! If I'm not around you —'

'Twins!' Mrs Mackie said, looming up behind our table. 'It's a little too early in the morning for us to listen to one of your rows. Perhaps you'd kindly keep them until you're on your own.'

Mrs Mackie still had power — even out of Park Wood. The twins stopped arguing and contented themselves by pulling horrible faces at each other.

'Now, what's all this ridiculous nonsense I've heard about a message from the ghost?' Mrs Mackie said.

'Oooh! It came into our dorm last night, Mrs Mackie,' Cerise said eagerly, 'and it was me who set it off because I'm a side-kick.'

'Psychic, you dope!' Erica said, and we all laughed.

'Dear me, Cerise, you'll be putting on a pair of gold hoop earrings and telling fortunes next,' Mrs Mackie said.

We met Gnome on the mountain at ten o'clock, as usual, and he took us to another part ('ze west slope,' as he called it) to go up on a different lift. I started to get into a bit of a panic just thinking about it, but to my relief found it was just a long line of little cars, each holding two people, going round and round forever up and down the mountain, and you just had to jump in and sit down. There was nothing even I could do wrong.

Apparently they stopped going round and round at five o'clock, when everyone had to come down from the mountains, and there were dire tales going about of someone who'd jumped in the last car, unseen by the man at the top, and, when the machinery stopped, had been left dangling in the car overnight.

Fleur told me the tale in a doom-laden voice when we were actually inside one and going up. 'The car was hanging over a ravine so the man inside couldn't jump,' she said in the voice she used for ghost stories. 'He was left there all night and froze to death! When the cars started up again the next morning in he came in his, frozen as hard as a lemon ice pop.'

'I don't believe it!' I said. 'And why a lemon ice pop, anyway?'

'Poetic licence,' Fleur said, 'you can say orange ice pop if you like. And it's all perfectly true – Cerise told me and you know she's a sidekick,' she added.

Skiing wasn't too bad – I was getting quite good at picking myself up and brushing the snow off quickly so that it didn't sink into my clothes. We were just about to go off for lunch when Gnome said he'd meet us at two o'clock by the button lift, near the coffee bar, and we'd go up to another slope for our afternoon's lesson.

Fleur shouted quickly, 'I bags not to go on the lift with Mickey!'

Well, I was quite hurt – especially when a few other voices said, not being funny but *they* didn't want to go with me, either.

'Sorry, Mickey,' Lorna said, 'but you are a bit of a disaster area on snow, aren't you?'

Gnome waved his fat little hands. 'Eet is only a one-person lift; we go in singles! When we go on the T-bar again, do not worry – I will go with Mickee!'

Everyone started laughing then and saying, 'Teacher's pet!' and all that, when Philippa suddenly yelled, 'Quickly! Miss Hermitage and Mr Lloyd are going past holding hands!'

Well, we all turned to look – including Gnome ('Who is zis peoples holding hands?') and Mouse and Fleur ski'd off a little way to see better, and somehow, on the way, Mouse hit a tree stump and went head over heels into a snowdrift.

This was nothing unusual as we were all falling down all the time, but this time she let out a big yell (big for her, anyway) and didn't get up.

Gnome was over there like a flash. He took both her skis off and loosened her boots, whilst we all stood round gawping and asking where it hurt.

It was obvious that it really *did* hurt. Mouse's face had gone completely white and although she tried to answer us, she just murmured something which no one could catch and then fainted.

'I think we 'ave some damage,' Gnome said seriously. 'I think maybe ze ankle is twisted badly, perhaps broken.'

It all got quite exciting after that – though not for Mouse. Erica, as the best skier amongst us, was dispatched to the first-aid post. They sent down two men and poor Mouse was loaded on to a stretcher and taken down in the cable car to go off to hospital. We looked around for one of the teachers but unfortunately could only find Mrs Taylor (poor Mouse again), so she went with her.

By the time all this had been sorted out, Mouse (now recovered from the faint and trying to be brave) had gone off and we'd had our lunch, we'd missed part of our afternoon lesson. Much to my relief, then, we didn't have to try out the new one-person lift, we just ski'd around by the restaurant and Gnome taught us first aid and safety precautions – including what to do if we were skiing with someone who broke something.

After the lesson we went back to the hostel, had baths, ate something which we decided was rat casserole and, at about seven o'clock, Mouse was brought back from hospital on crutches – with a great big plaster cast on her leg.

'D'you know the last thing my dad said to me?' she asked us with a grin. 'Don't break your leg!'

At eight o'clock, when everyone in the hostel had covered the plaster cast with drawings, signatures and rude poems (written very small so Mrs Mackie couldn't see them), Mouse had a visitor: Gnome.

'Eet is too bad,' he said, shaking his head so that the end of his bobble hat bobbed up and down. 'Ze season is nearly over and I think I have got away with eet, I think that this year no one in my classes has any broken boneses, then . . .' He gave an expressive shrug and pulled out a box of chocolates from behind his back which he presented to Mouse.

'Well!' Cerise said when Gnome had gone off to talk to the teachers and we were falling upon the chocolates. 'Do you think that the ski instructors visit everyone who breaks their leg?'

'Why? Are you thinking of breaking a couple so that Mr Supercool will visit *you*?' Fleur asked, and before we could laugh Cerise said, 'Well, I might . . .'

At about ten o'clock we all went to bed. Mrs Mackie came up to help get Mouse settled, and we promised to help her get dressed in the morning.

At about half-past ten we were still wide-awake and chatting (Cerise was telling us what it felt like to be so mad about someone that you couldn't eat and Fleur said with the food we got here she didn't see it made any difference) when some invitations came under our door, written on the back of our ghosty party ones. They said:

MISSION IMPOSSIBLE! AN INVITATION FROM ROOM 8! DARE YOU TO COME TO A MIDNIGHT FEAST AND DO DARING AND DANGEROUS DEEDS!

PS – Owing to difficult circumstances (Alison) the midnight feast will be held in Room 3.

At eleven o'clock, Su, Erica and the twins turned up saying they couldn't be bothered to wait until midnight. They were closely followed by Alice, saying, 'We'll get into terrible trouble! I really shouldn't be here, you know!' and 'What if we're caught!' over and over again.

We sat around Mouse's bed, ate the rest of her chocolates, some jelly beans and a few dry biscuits which the twins had found somewhere, and then Erica pulled out an envelope from under her dressing gown.

'Mission impossible!' she said dramatically. 'There are twelve of us, and in here are twelve pieces of paper, some blank, and some with a daring deed which must be performed. Everyone has to draw out one piece of paper and, if it has a daring deed on it, carry it out.'

'How can I carry out a daring deed sitting here?' Mouse wanted to know.

'In your case a person of your choice will do the deed for you,' Erica said.

'I mustn't do a daring deed!' Alice said in a fearful voice. 'I'd get into terrible trouble . . . my sister was Head Girl here and I'm going to be one, too.'

'It's the luck of the draw!' Erica said. 'If you've come along to the Mission Impossible Midnight Feast, then you must obey the rules.'

'Oh, I don't . . .' Alice began, but Erica shook the envelope up and down under her nose.

'Take one!' she commanded, and Alice meekly put her hand in the envelope, pulled out a folded piece of paper and opened it.

'It's a blank!' she said in relief.

The envelope was passed to the rest of us and I got a blank too (I was quite disappointed) while Cerise announced in a frightened voice that she had to steal a piece of cheese from the kitchens, Arina had to knot the laces on Alison's moon boots together so that when she put them on she fell over and Fleur – well, when she read hers she burst out laughing.

'Great!' she said. 'Just what I could do with!'

'What you you got?' I asked.

'Taking a person of my choice,' she said, poking me in the ribs, 'I've got to creep out of the hostel and come back with a takeaway pizza!'

'Extra large size – enough for everyone!' Erica said.

'Let's go, then!' Fleur said, rushing to get into her jeans. 'Come on, Mickey!'

The doors to the hostel seemed to be open all night so I suppose we could have just crept past reception and out of the front door, but that wasn't exciting enough for Fleur, she wanted to do it properly.

'We must knot the sheets together and get out of the window!' she said.

'But we're on the ground floor!'

'Never mind! They always do it like that in books.'

The others helped – we didn't actually knot the sheets together because they would have been too long – but they held one end of a sheet and we used it to climb out.

Keeping well in to the sides of the road, although we needn't have bothered because no one took the slightest bit of notice of us, we made our way down to the town. We knew where the takeaway pizza place was because we'd eaten there once after skiing, but we weren't sure if we had enough money for the biggest size. Our pocket money was dished out daily and we'd already bought apple strudels at tea time.

'Might have to be the medium deep pan,' Fleur said, looking up at the prices as we went in counting through our francs. 'Shall we get the veggie one or one with ham?' she asked me, but for an answer I just gave a frightened squeal.

'What's up?' she asked, and I pointed. There, standing right by the counter waiting for their order, were Mr Lloyd and Miss Hermitage! He had his arm round her and they were looking into each other's eye's in a silly sort of way.

'Quick! Get out!' Fleur said, tugging at my arm, but just as we were about to make a dash for the door, Mr Lloyd turned and saw us, then nudged Miss Hermitage to look, too.

For a moment no one moved or said anything, and then Mr Lloyd strolled up to us and said, 'Well, girls, what d'you think you're doing out so late at night?'

'Er . . . we were hungry,' I said.

'Starving!' Fleur added. 'Practically dead with starvation.'

There was the glimmer of a smile on Miss Hermitage's face. 'I see,' she said. She looked at Mr Lloyd. 'What are we going to do with them, Barney?'

'We're really sorry. We'll never come out again at night!' I said.

'We only did it because it was either that or starve to death!' Fleur added.

Mr Lloyd raised his eyebrows. 'Well, girls,' he said, 'let's put it this way. You don't tell Mrs Mackie about seeing us and we won't tell her about seeing you. All right?'

'Right!' we echoed, relieved.

'Go straight back now and we'll forget about it,' Miss Hermitage said. 'And don't leave the hostel again!'

'Of course not! Thanks!' Fleur and I said together.

'Er ... can we just go and get our pizza first?' I asked – and they actually let us!

We zoomed back to the hostel and in through our window in record time and, whilst cutting up tiny slices of pizza for everyone with Cerise's nail file, told our adventure.

'*Two* adventures!' I said. While we'd been out the other daring deeds had been done, and Cerise had the smallest piece of cheese anyone had ever seen to prove it.

It was nearly twelve-thirty by then.

'And no ghost!' Erica said, disappointed.

'We'd better go to bed,' Alice said – she'd worn her worried, anxious look all night – 'otherwise we'll be too tired to ski in the morning.'

'Just a sec!' Mouse said. 'I took a piece of paper and I got a daring deed, too.'

'I was waiting for someone to own up to having another one!' Erica said with a grin.

Mouse waved her piece of paper. 'This is a great one! The person chosen has to go to Mrs Mackie's room, steal a pair of her knickers and put them on the mayor's statue outside the hostel!'

We all roared with laughter.

'What a scream!' I said. 'What a good idea!'

'I'm glad you think it's so good, Mickey,' Mouse giggled, 'because I've chosen you to do it for me!'

Chapter Seven

THURSDAY: CERISE TRIES TO
BREAK HER LEG

'Are you sure you'll be all right?' we asked
Mouse, after propping her up outside the
hostel on a chair with a mountain of
pillows.

'Course!' she said cheerfully. 'My leg
doesn't hurt at all now it's all done up. To
tell you the truth, I wasn't all that struck
on skiing anyway. As we did more things
I was beginning to get a bit scared.'

'I'd be more scared staying here!' Cerise
said. 'Suppose the ghost arrives while we're
all out!'

'Don't be ridiculous,' Philippa said. 'Who-
ever heard of a ghost appearing during
the day?'

'You never know!' Cerise said, pulling up the collar of her skiing jacket and looking about her fearfully.

'I'll be quite happy staying here reading books and getting nice and brown,' Mouse said. She nodded towards the statue of the mayor and lowered her voice. 'If I get bored I'll amuse myself imagining how he'll look tomorrow with Mrs Mackie's knickers on his head.'

I grinned at Mouse. 'Mmm . . . thanks a lot for giving me that little job!'

'You'll love it!' Fleur chipped in.

'If you're so sure of that then you can help me!' I said.

Lorna sped over to us. 'We're allowed to come back here at lunchtime if we want,' she reported. 'Mrs Mackie says it'll break Mouse's day up a bit.'

'You don't have to . . .' Mouse began, but most of us said we would.

'It'll be something to do,' Fleur said. 'We'll bring you a pizza from the take-away. *Another* pizza.'

Mouse waved as our bus went down the street and we all waved back. I felt quite envious. Not of the broken leg, I didn't want one of those, but of the fact that she could just sit there all day and do absolutely nothing. She didn't have to kill her feet in horrible heavy boots, she didn't have to keep falling over, she didn't have to ski on one leg ('just so our legses get used to it') or make a complete idiot of herself trying to get on a lift . . .

I wasn't really complaining – I was having a great time – but as far as I was concerned it would have been even better without the skiing.

The lift that Gnome had called the button lift was just as bad as I'd feared. It consisted of a strap hanging down from a big overhead pulley thing that you grabbed hold of, swung between your legs and then just hung on to for dear life. As well as hanging on you also had to keep your skis steady, hold on to your poles, gloves, goggles and try and steer yourself in a straight line. If you wandered off the main runway bit you went over half-buried sticks or rocks which made you wobbly or tipped you up.

After about six tries I managed to get on and stay on – and then halfway up I dropped a glove, bent over to retrieve it and wobbled myself off the pulley flat on to the snow. I just lay there, scared to move in case the next person coming along ran me over. It was Alison and she did try to, but she couldn't do it properly without coming off the track herself, so instead she went past telling me how stupid I looked.

Once I'd been rescued – twice – and

we were all at the top, Gnome started to teach us parallel turns. It all looked much too complicated for me, though. I just couldn't get the hang of the bit where you had to snap your top ski round to meet the bottom one, so I spent a long time pretending to get my boots just right and adjusting and readjusting my bindings. Anyway, as soon as someone had slowly parallel-turned right down to the bottom of the slope, they had to get the button lift up again, so as far as I was concerned, the least number of times I did it the better.

Just before lunch Gnome asked if anyone wanted to go in for the beginners' bronze medal the following day, our last day's skiing, and a few said they'd try.

'Why don't you have a go?' Fleur urged me. 'It's really easy – it's not timed or anything, you've just got to finish the course.'

'No fear,' I said. 'I'd fall over as soon as they said the word "go". Skiing doesn't seem to be my thing,' I added resignedly. The truth was, I didn't seem to *have* a thing – or if I did, it was a jolly long time getting itself discovered.

At lunchtime nearly everyone went back to see Mouse. Gnome came with us, too, and he treated her to a pizza.

'Well!' Cerise said indignantly when she

saw him sitting there chatting away. 'Talk about favouritism!'

'I expect all the instructors are like that with anyone who hurts themselves,' Alice said. 'After all, we're their responsibility, aren't we?'

'Mmm ... suppose so,' Cerise said, before going into the hostel to reapply her sunblock, refluff her hair and think of new ways of trying to get the attention of Mr Supercool.

After an afternoon of more parallel turns and more wobbling dangerously on the button lift, Fleur and I reported back to a teacher and then ski'd very cautiously to the big cable car which would take us down the mountain. The more experienced skiers went all the way down on skis, of course, but we certainly weren't attempting that – we weren't allowed to, for a start.

We queued for about ten minutes and were almost at the front ready to go in the next lift when I heard a little cry for help. A little, squeaky, Cerise sort of cry.

'It *is* Cerise, isn't it?' Fleur said, and we lost our places in the queue and fought our way back to see what was up. Sure enough, at the back, sitting on the hard-packed snow and looking pathetic, was Cerise – and Mrs Taylor had just reached her.

'Whatever is it?' Mrs Taylor asked.

'I just stumbled on a mogul!' Cerise said, her lower lip trembling pathetically.

'Really?' Mrs Taylor said. 'I don't see any moguls. Certainly not near here.'

'It was over there!' Cerise said, pointing nowhere in particular. 'I fell really heavily and I heard a loud cracking noise. I think I've broken my leg!'

'Oooh, you . . . !' I said before I could stop myself, and Fleur nudged me hard.

Mrs Taylor knew Cerise well, though — it had been *her* who'd made Cerise and Philippa lose the only housepoints in the history of the first year.

'Well, let's see if you can stand on it,' she said now in her no-nonsense voice.

'I c . . . can't,' Cerise said. 'It's too painful. I might faint.'

'Up you get!' Mrs Taylor said bracingly. 'If you faint I shall catch you.'

Cerise looked around her, dismayed. There was only one person *she* wanted to catch her.

'Could . . . could you tell my skiing instructor I've broken my leg,' she managed to stammer out.

'The first thing to do is to ascertain if you've done so,' Mrs Taylor said sharply. 'Up you get!'

Putting a hand under Cerise's arm, she helped her to her feet. 'Awaagh!' Cerise

yelled, screwing up her eyes. 'The pain!'
She opened her eyes and looked at me.
'Go and get Jean-Paul,' she said in a faint
whisper.

But I took one look at Mrs Taylor's face
and didn't dare move.

'It's not swollen,' Mrs Taylor said, bending over to loosen Cerise's boot and prod-
ding her foot a bit. 'Looks quite normal,
actually. Are you sure it's painful?' Cerise
gave a dreadful moan by way of an answer.
'We'll take you down, I think, and see what
Miss Hermitage says.'

Cerise moaned again, her eyes darting
about in the crowd. She was obviously
hoping that Mr Supercool would suddenly
appear and take over.

'Take an arm each, you two girls,' Mrs
Taylor said briskly, 'and I'll carry Cerise's
equipment.'

The crowd parted as we half-carried
Cerise through to the cable car.

'You old fraud! You're only pretending,'
Fleur whispered in her ear. 'You just want
old Supercool to come swanning about with
boxes of chocolates.'

'I don't!' Cerise said indignantly, forgetting her pained and suffering expression.
'I'm absolutely ... awaagh ... crippled
with pain.'

'We don't believe a word of it!' Fleur said.

'It's the right foot you've broken, remember,' I hissed in her other ear. 'Don't get them mixed up.'

Mrs Taylor watched Cerise closely all the way back to the hostel but – maybe she'd been taking acting lessons from Jane or something – she didn't let her suffering expression slip again. Every so often she'd give a quick 'Awaagh!' if she didn't think we were taking enough notice of her.

Back in Dorm 3 she was laid out on the bed, and an amused Mouse hobbled in to watch. Miss Hermitage arrived back from the mountain, removed both of Cerise's boots and announced that there was no swelling to be seen.

'There's not even any sign of a muscle injury. Perhaps you've just bruised it,' she said.

'No, I haven't,' Cerise said crossly. 'It's broken, I tell you. It's a very small break – sort of inside so you can't feel it.'

'Well, we'll just see how it goes, shall we?' Miss Hermitage said smoothly. 'We'll bind it up now and see how you feel in the morning.'

It was bound up with much fuss, and the stretch bandage secured with a cerise-coloured plastic brooch in the shape of an alsatian dog.

Even this didn't console her, though. She was most put-out about the whole thing.

'If I say my leg's broken, then it's broken,' she said when Miss Hermitage had gone. 'What does she know about it?'

'Well, she's our PE teacher and she's had nursing experience,' Lorna said.

'She wasn't in the least bit bothered about me!' Cerise grumbled. 'Bet she couldn't wait to get back to Mr Lloyd!'

Cerise borrowed one of Mouse's wooden crutches to get into the dining room, and then wished she hadn't bothered when we each found a sort of meat ball (reindeer meat, we decided) with a teaspoon of rice waiting for us.

After dinner we sat around in the lounge chatting and trying to decide what to do that evening. Fleur and I discussed whether to do the Mission Impossible knicker run early, or wait until the teachers had gone to bed. Every so often Cerise would limp to one of the windows and look out, then wistfully sigh and come back and sit with us again. When Gnome called by to see how Mouse was once more, Cerise went quite pink with indignation.

'I'm phoning home!' she said. 'I've got emergency money to ring any time I want. I'm going to talk to Mummy and tell her that my leg's broken and they won't do anything about it! It's not fair. It's . . .'

She stopped as Mrs Mackie came into the lounge smiling and carrying a clip board. 'Good news!' she said. 'I've been ringing round the tour companies and I've managed to get us all on a sleigh ride tonight.'

'What's a sleigh like?' Philippa asked.

'Well, they're big open coaches drawn by horses holding about thirty people,' Mrs Mackie explained. 'They usually have three or four going along behind each other, all with bells on, and they drive through all the little villages. Everyone wraps rugs round themselves and sings – it's great fun!'

Mrs Mackie said that Mouse had been booked on a seat next to a driver so she could stretch her leg out.

'What about the Mission Impossible, though?' Fleur whispered.

'We'll have to do it tomorrow,' I whispered back, 'when Mrs Mackie's out.'

'Awaggh!' called Cerise – she'd been ignored for at least five minutes.

'Will you be joining us, Cerise?' Mrs Mackie asked pleasantly.

Cerise rolled her eyes to try and give an impression of intense and horrible pain. 'I'd like to,' she said hoarsely, 'but my leg's too bad. Couldn't put weight on it . . .'

Mrs Mackie shook her head. 'Pity,' she

said. 'It's a lovely trip. Of course, I didn't manage to get the four sleighs for our exclusive use ...' she consulted her clip board '... so we've got to share with a Merideth Boys' School. It'll be nearly as good, though.'

I think Cerise had been about to make another strangled cry, but at the magic word 'boys' it froze on her lips. Instead she bent over and gave her ankle a vigorous rub.

'Coming to get ready, everyone?' Annabel called. 'Are we allowed to take blankets off our beds to wrap ourselves in, Mrs Mackie?'

'Don't you dare! Rugs will be supplied,' Mrs Mackie said.

'See you later, Cerise!' we called.

Cerise had been staring down at her leg, very hard, and now she stuck it out in front of her and wriggled her foot a bit.

'Do you know,' she said, 'my leg doesn't feel too bad at all now.'

Mrs Mackie went to stand by her. 'Are you sure, Cerise? I understood it was extremely painful.'

'It feels lots better now, though. I think I might be able to come.'

'Well!' Mrs Mackie said. 'Fancy that! It must be a miracle, mustn't it?'

'Yes, I suppose it must,' Cerise said, and,

just limping very slightly, she made her way past us and upstairs.

Mrs Mackie paused in the doorway and spoke to the other teachers. 'Isn't it amazing what the mention of a boys' school can do?'

Fleur and I, who were last out of the door, laughed, and Mrs Mackie rolled her eyes at us. 'Between you and me I'm just profoundly grateful that Jane Hutt didn't come on this trip,' she said. 'One girl who thinks she's an actress is bad enough, without having a professional one here as well.'

The sleigh ride was lovely. The bells on the horses' bridles rang, everyone sang and the people in the small and snowy villages we passed all waved to us. There was no boys' school, though. I don't know whether the whole thing had been a ploy on Mrs Mackie's part or if they just didn't turn up, but anyhow Cerise was walking properly on her leg by then and it was too late to go back to pretending that it was broken.

When we arrived back it was gone eleven and we went straight to our dorms, all really tired. We weren't having a midnight feast that night – and I couldn't have gone on any impossible missions if you'd paid me.

Cerise, first in our dorm, ran in and ran straight out again with a yelp.

'Not another broken leg,' Philippa said wearily.

'No, another ghost!' Cerise said.

Warily, we looked round the door. The beds had all been pushed to the centre of the room, and there was a message on the mirror saying:

THE GHOST WALKS AGAIN!

Chapter Eight

FRIDAY: CONCERNING MRS MACKIE'S UNMENTIONABLES

'How are we going to do it?' I said to Fleur as the cable car started off up the mountain.

'Get a bronze medal?' Fleur asked. 'I thought you weren't going to try for it?'

'I'm not,' I said. 'I don't mean that, I mean . . .' I looked round cautiously then added in a whisper, '. . . get Mrs Mackie's knickers.'

'Oh, *them*,' Fleur said. 'That's up to you. I mean, it's your Mission Impossible, isn't it? I'm just going along for the ride.'

'You will come with me though, won't you?'

'Course!' It was her turn to look around us uneasily. 'You do think it'll be all right creeping around the corridors at midnight? You don't think there's anything in this ghost business?'

'Course not! It's just one of the second-years having a joke. Or Alison.'

'What's that?' a voice said gruffly, and we looked round, startled, to see that Alison was squashed nearby. The cable car was so crowded that we hadn't noticed.

'Oh, nothing,' I said quickly.

'You two are up to something,' Alison said, narrowing her piggy eyes. 'Don't think I haven't seen you whispering in corners, plotting.'

Fleur gave Alison her sunniest smile. 'Us? Plotting?'

'Something's going on, I know it is. Something to do with Mrs Mackie. You think you're really clever, don't you? I suppose you even think you've managed to keep your stupid midnight feasts a secret from everyone!'

Fleur and I, with difficulty because it was such a tight squeeze in there, both turned our backs on her.

'You're not allowed to leave your dorms at night,' Alison said. 'The teachers said there would be strict penalties; they'd stop anyone skiing if they were found out.'

'Oh no!' I said in mock fright. 'I hope they don't stop us skiing tomorrow!'

'Yes, well, you just want to be careful someone doesn't report you,' Alison hissed.

'If they stop us skiing tomorrow ...' Fleur said in a desperate voice – but with a wink at me.

'If they do ...' I said, 'I wouldn't be at all surprised – seeing as we're going to be sitting on a coach all day!'

'And it's a bit difficult skiing on one of those!'

'Although you could try snow-ploughing up and down the aisles,' I added, and then we both burst out giggling.

Alison's face went red. 'Oh, you think you're so clever, don't you?' she exploded. 'Just you watch it, that's all. You watch that one of the teachers doesn't find out about your stupid feasts and your stupid dares.'

Fleur and I raised our eyebrows at each other. While we'd been having midnight feasts Alison had obviously been listening at doors. And all the time we'd thought she was asleep!

We reached the top and the girls who were going to try for the bronze medal went off with Mr Lloyd. Cerise and the ones who were trying for their silver went off with Miss Hermitage and the rest of us went to our normal classes. Cerise, of course, had completely recovered from her 'broken leg', but in a last-ditch attempt to win the heart of Mr Supercool was wearing a pink and silver embroidered waistcoat over her cerise ski outfit.

The morning's skiing went on as usual, although I had a really dippy day, falling over twice as much, going out of control every five minutes, sliding into trees and altogether being completely useless.

'No matter,' Gnome said, shaking his head so that the tail of his hat swung from side to side, 'Everyone she have ze bad day sometimes, but after ze bad day always comes ze good day.'

'Not for me,' I said. 'For me, after ze bad day skiing comes ze next bad day. Anyway, we're going home tomorrow. My next bad day will be next year.'

'You come again?' Gnome asked.

I nodded. 'I might gently twist my ankle on the first day, though, so I can't ski.'

Gnome looked at me, puzzled, and then he slapped his forehead. 'Oh, you make ze joke!'

'Sort of,' I said.

We met up with everyone else in the restaurant at lunchtime. Cerise and Annabel had got their silver medals and were proudly wearing them over their ski jackets, and Fleur and the others had all got their bronzes.

'You should have tried for it,' Fleur said to me, breathing on hers and trying to make it shiny. 'Everyone got one – even if they fell over. I fell over twice!'

I looked at her medal wistfully – it would have been nice to have one to show off to my brothers. 'Would you still get one if you came down the entire run on your bottom, though?' I asked.

'Probably not,' Fleur said. 'And it's just as well that you didn't try, because you also had to show that you could negotiate a lift.'

'That would have been me out straight away, then,' I said, relieved that I hadn't gone for it.

After our baths that evening, we started packing. This didn't take long as it was just a case of throwing everything back in our cases – I even remembered to screw up my vests to make them look worn.

'Last midnight feast tonight, then?' Philippa said.

I nodded. 'Have we got anything to eat?'

She pulled a face. 'Don't think so. And no one's got any money to buy anything, either.' Her face suddenly cleared. 'Except Annabel! She arrived with about four times as much spending money as anyone else.'

'I thought Mrs Mackie took it?'

'She did. I expect she'd let her have it back on the last night, though.'

She went off to arrange things and I thought about the Mission Impossible knicker run. It had to be completed; we'd never live it down otherwise.

After dinner – the smallest chicken leg anyone had ever seen (canary, we decided), Cerise tore into the lounge waving something in the air.

'A postcard from Araminta!' she shrieked. 'They had it behind the reception desk. A postcard from Araminta!'

We all pretended not to be interested – especially Philippa, Cerise's main rival for our resident superstar's affections. A postcard from Jane would probably just be a list of all the exciting things she was doing while we were away: auditions attended, contracts signed, garden fêtes opened and so on.

'She says I've got to forget all about Jean-Paul, that he sounds much too old for me,' Cerise read out to us. Her voice rose excitedly, 'She says she's going to fix me up with someone from *Village Life* instead! And . . .' she squealed, '. . . she says she's going to meet the ferry! Her publicity agent wants some shots of her greeting her school friends off the boat!'

She sank down on to the arm of a chair, fanning herself with the postcard, quite overcome. 'I wonder who it is on *Village*

Life? I hope it's not that new postman's son. What shall I wear when we get off the ferry? They're bound to want some close-ups of Araminta's best friend.' She shot a triumphant look at Philippa, who was pretending to read a notice on the wall written in French. 'Luckily I've got this really amazing pink silk blouse with me. I shall change into it on the boat.'

When Cerise had read out the postcard a few more times so that we knew it by heart, we settled down to write up the log books of our daily activities we were supposed to keep. A bit later the teachers came in and got us playing a quiz they'd prepared with forfeits and penalties for the wrong answers. After that we had a few mad games of cards, then Mr Lloyd said he thought we ought to get an earlyish night.

Everyone put out a few mild groans – we felt it was expected of us. 'But it's our last night!' Erica said.

'Don't forget you've got an early start and then we'll be travelling all day,' Mrs Mackie reminded her.

'Are all the teachers going to bed too?' I asked innocently.

'Never you mind!' she said. 'Suffice to say that we teachers don't need quite as much sleep as you.'

'And we need some time off after putting up with you lot all day!' Mr Lloyd added.

Feigning reluctance, we went upstairs where we all goggled at the amount of food Annabel had managed to buy: cakes, rolls, chocolate biscuits, crisps – even two cold pizzas.

'We'll let Alison go to sleep and then come along to your dorm,' Su said to me. 'Will you have got the knickers by then?'

'Don't know,' I said, pulling a face. As far as I was concerned, the closer it came to the time I had to get them, the more impossible it seemed – which was what Erica had intended, of course. As dares went, though, it seemed to me to be worth at least five getting-cheese-from-the-kitchens.

'I think we ought to wear balaclavas,' Fleur said later when we were in our nighties and dressing gowns, preparing to set off. 'Then if anyone sees us, they won't know who we are.'

'Why don't you disguise yourselves?' Cerise said. 'Wear someone else's ski clothes, for instance.'

Fleur and I looked at each other and rolled our eyes. 'Good idea,' I said. 'Can I borrow your ski suit then, Cerise?'

'But everyone knows mine is . . .' she began, and then giggled.

'Exactly!' I said.

When Philippa heard the teachers going upstairs, I followed them at a distance – they went into Mrs Taylor's room. Creeping up to the door, I heard the chink of glasses and laughter; it sounded as if they were about to play charades or something.

I went back to Fleur. 'They're in Mrs Taylor's room,' I said. 'Are you ready? This is it.'

Solemnly, we shook hands all round the room. 'If we never return, let our parents know what happened to us,' I said.

'If we never return,' Fleur echoed, 'you, Cerise, may have my bronze medal.'

'I've already got a silver one!' she said indignantly.

'And you, Annabel, may look after my gerbil.'

'I'm allergic to them!'

'Hurry back!' Mouse said, sitting up in bed looking half frightened for us and half gleeful that she'd broken her leg and didn't have to do this most impossible of Mission Impossibles.

We went out of the dorm softly and silently.

'Keep close to the walls,' Fleur said in a whisper, 'if you see anyone, pretend to be foreign. Say you do nit spik English.'

'That won't work very well if it's one of our own teachers!'

'Ssh!' she said. 'A noise!' There was a clanking sound from further down the corridor and we looked at each other. 'The ghost!' she said.

I began to giggle. 'Daft! It's just someone coming up in the lift!'

'Quickly! Get into the cupboard!' she said, and she opened the door of what turned out to be a linen cupboard. Bending double, we pushed ourselves in and waited for a man with suitcases – a new guest probably – to pass by.

'Knowing my luck, the door will jam and we'll be in here all night and miss all that food,' I whispered, but the person passed, the door opened and we were out in the corridor again.

I grabbed Fleur's hand and we tiptoed along the corridor towards Mrs Mackie's room. I tried the handle – it wasn't locked – and we went in!

'We'll get absolutely killed if anyone finds out!' Fleur said suddenly. 'Expelled, probably.'

'No one's going to find out!' I said, but I was so scared my voice was all shaky. 'Quickly, where d'you think her underwear will be?'

We dived towards the top drawer of the

cupboard next to her bed, but there was nothing in it. We looked further down: all the drawers were empty!

'I bet she's done all her packing and everything's in her suitcase!' Fleur said. 'What'll we do now?'

'Find the suitcase!' I said.

It was on the other side of the bed – and locked!

'That's that, then,' Fleur said. 'Let's go!'

'We can't!' I said. 'The others will never let us forget it. Fancy having a Mission Impossible that *was* impossible.'

'That's too bad,' Fleur said, 'let's just get out of here!'

I popped my head round the door of her bathroom. 'I'll just have a quick look in here.'

'Come on!' Fleur said urgently.

I made a grab at something white and frilly on a radiator. 'I've got some!' I yelped. 'She left them on a radiator!'

'Great. Now let's go!'

We sped silently downstairs towards our dorm.

'Let's put them on the statue now,' Fleur said breathlessly when we reached the bottom of the stairs. 'Then we haven't got to go out again.'

Getting outside was easy – we just used

the side door. Climbing on the statue was easy, too, but then when it came to putting the knickers on the statue, we hit a snag. They weren't knickers!

I held the offending garment out towards Fleur in dismay. 'It's a shower cap!' I said. 'Plastic lace ... I thought it was frilly knickers.'

'You might have known Mrs Mackie wouldn't have *those*,' Fleur said.

'What'll we do now, then?'

Fleur shrugged. 'Nothing. No one will know, will they? We won't say anything, we'll just go ahead and bung it on the mayor's head.'

I brightened up. 'It might even be better,' I said. 'If something dreadful happens and Mrs Mackie finds out, she won't go so mad as if we'd taken a pair of her knickers.'

'Quite,' said Fleur.

Mission accomplished, we went in the side door and began to make our way back to our room.

'There's someone coming!' I said suddenly, hearing a door opening and closing. 'Not the ghost?!'

We hid in a doorway. It wasn't a ghost, though, but the sturdy form of Alison, dressing gown firmly pulled around her, making her way up the stairs to the teachers' rooms.

'Bet she's going to tell on us!' I whispered.

'Follow her!'

Hardly able to breathe for the excitement of it all, we shadowed Alison to Mrs Taylor's room. She knocked on the door and asked for Mrs Mackie.

'I thought you ought to know,' we heard her saying, 'that all the girls in my dorm have disappeared – just gone off somewhere. They've done it before, as well.'

'I see,' Mrs Mackie said in a stern voice. 'And why have you come to tell me, Alison?'

'Because you said no one was to leave their rooms,' Alison said in her most smarmy voice. 'And something else is going on, too,' she added, 'something in Dorm 3 to do with Michelle and Fleur. I heard them planning something this morning. They said . . .'

'Yes. Thank you, Alison,' Mrs Mackie said. 'I'm sure it's just something that happens here every year – just some sort of harmless midnight feast.'

'But you said . . .'

'And why do you think you haven't been included in these night-time high jinks?'

'I don't know, Mrs Mackie.'

'Because, I'm afraid, no one likes a sneak,

110

Alison. And that's what you are, aren't you?'

'Well, I . . .' Alison mumbled.

Fleur and I clutched each other with glee.

'As a matter of fact, I shall be waking up all the girls soon,' Mrs Mackie went on. 'We've a little surprise planned for you all. So go back to your room now and let's hope that the other girls don't find out that you were . . . er . . . *ratting* on them, I believe they call it now.'

'But, Mrs Mackie . . .' we heard Alison say before we started running as quickly as we could down the stairs and back to our dorm. The room 8 girls were there waiting.

'Did you do it?' Arina asked excitedly.

'Bet you didn't!' said Philippa.

'Yes, we did, but never mind that now!' I said, pulling off my dressing gown and running across the room.

'Quickly!' Fleur yelled, leaping for her bed. 'Hide the midnight feast and get into your beds!'

'Go back to your own dorm!' I said to Erica and the others. 'Mrs Mackie's coming to wake you up!'

In a split second they'd all disappeared. We got into our beds and pulled the clothes up to our chins and a few moments later

Mrs Mackie tapped on the door and came in.

'Ah, all sleeping peacefully, I see!' she said in a voice which meant she knew quite well that we weren't. 'Sorry to wake you, girls, but we've got a surprise for you.'

Sleepily, hiding our grins, we sat up and rubbed our eyes. Fleur gave a brilliantly authentic yawn, I stretched and pretended not to know where I was. I was going to say, 'Am I dreaming?' in a dozy voice but I thought that might be carrying things too far.

'What is it, Mrs Mackie?' Lorna asked.

'Nothing to worry about,' she said. 'It's just that every Friday night the people of the village arrange a torch-lit descent of the mountain for advanced skiers. We didn't say anything about it earlier, because we wanted you to get a couple of hours' sleep, but we've arranged for all our party to go into the hotel dining room and watch.'

Grinning widely at each other, we all got up and put on our dressing gowns. Mouse and her leg were manoeuvred out of bed by Mrs Mackie and a big furry sock was put on the toes which were sticking out of her plaster cast.

'There's a hot lemonade punch for those

who want it,' Mrs Mackie said, 'and sausages on sticks and things. It'll be a midnight feast. That'll be fun, won't it?' she added, smiling.

'Lovely! Make a nice change,' I said, nudging Fleur.

'Something really different,' Fleur added, nudging me back.

'Oh, Mrs Mackie,' Annabel asked, 'I've bought some food for the . . . er . . . journey. Can I bring it along?'

'Of course – as long as you don't mind sharing it,' Mrs Mackie said. She really wasn't such a bad old stick.

We all went to the dining room, which gave a lovely view of the nearest – and tallest – mountain. At the top were tiny little pin-pricks of flickering light, which Miss Hermitage explained were the ski instructors (a sigh from Cerise) and other advanced skiers. As we watched, sipping our lemonade punch and munching our sausages and midnight feast, they began to ski down the mountain in a continuous trail, in and out of the fir trees, each holding a flaming torch aloft.

'Magical!' Miss Lemming said, and then turned to Cerise, who'd started sniffing. 'Do you want a hanky, dear? It's beautiful, isn't it? And it does make one feel rather emotional.'

'It's not that,' Cerise snuffled, 'it's just that one of those little points of light is Jean-Paul and I'm never going to see him again. Never!' And, holding her hand to her forehead, she gave a muffled sob.

'She's been having acting lessons from Jane,' I whispered to Fleur.

Chapter Nine
SATURDAY: HOME!

'I'm afraid we're up before the staff and much too early for breakfast this morning,' Miss Hermitage said as we gathered, bleary-eyed, in the hostel lounge.

'Well, that's a relief,' I said to Fleur.

'Best news this holiday!'

'But the hostel has kindly arranged for packed breakfasts to be left on the coaches,' she continued.

Fleur and I looked at each other but were too tired even to raise a groan.

'Now has everyone got absolutely everything out of their dorms?' Miss Lemming asked. 'There can be no turning back once we set off because we've got a very tight schedule to keep to.'

We all promised that we'd stripped our beds, thrown all our rubbish away and packed absolutely beautifully, forgetting nothing.

'The coaches will be here any minute,' she said, 'so perhaps you'd like to get into groups outside.'

We all went out – to be met by an excited group of second-years who were coming back in to tell everyone that the mayor's statue had a pair of knickers on its head!

'You did it, then!' Arina said to me. 'I didn't believe you had!'

'Of course we did!'

'No mission is too impossible for us,' Fleur added.

Lugging our cases, we went out and looked admiringly at the mayor.

'He looks quite fetching,' I said to Fleur, 'a shower cap suits him.'

'Hides his sticky-out ears,' she agreed.

Basking in the admiration of those-who-knew and enjoying the excited whispers of those-who-didn't, we got on the coach.

Breakfast was two dry slices of bread (very dry, because they'd been sitting on the coach waiting for us all night), a little plastic sachet of marmalade and a piece of dry cheese. We dropped our bread and cheese out of the window for the birds but opened our marmalade sachets and licked them clean. It was only six o'clock in the morning so we weren't hungry yet – especially after the feasting of the night before – and we also knew that we'd be having several stops on the journey where we'd be able to get hamburgers and chips and stuff.

'Miss Lemming! Mrs Mackie! Have you seen the statue has got knickers on?' Alison asked as soon as the teachers appeared. 'Whose do you think they are?' she added, looking slyly at me and Fleur.

'Knickers? What do you mean – instead of underpants?' Miss Lemming asked, and then peered out of the coach window. 'Oh – you mean on his head!'

Fleur and I nudged each other, waiting for Mrs Mackie to look and praying that she wouldn't recognise the mayor's headgear.

'How novel!' she said when she'd settled herself down and eventually looked out. 'Perhaps it's some quaint French custom.'

She looked closer, rubbing at the window. 'White lace . . . it looks remarkably like my shower cap!' she suddenly said. 'In fact I'm almost sure that . . .'

But with a roar the engine of the coach started up, Miss Lemming shouted, 'We're off, everyone!' and we all craned to look out

117

of the window and bid our last goodbyes to
the hostel.

'Goodbye!' we all yelled to no one in particular. 'See you again!'

'And goodbye Jean-Paul!' we heard Cerise
say in a heartbroken voice.

Mrs Mackie was still looking out of the
window. 'I couldn't find it this morning,
either,' she said. 'How very strange.' A
second or two later she asked in a startled
voice, 'Whatever's all that over the ground
outside the hostel?'

We looked back as we turned the corner:
the ground was thick with dry bread and
cheese slices.

'Where did all that lot come from? You
haven't all thrown your breakfasts out,
have you?'

We all looked at each other. 'Well, you're
always saying we should remember the
birds on cold mornings,' I said.

'So we all remembered them at the same
time,' said Erica.

'Very commendable, I'm sure,' Mrs Mackie
said. 'But about that shower cap – if it *is* a
shower cap . . .'

'Perhaps it was the ghost who did it!'
Arina said.

'But I don't believe in ghosts, Jasbir.'

'I'm Arina!' Arina said, grinning – the
teachers had been getting them wrong all

week. 'And nor do I believe in real ghosts –
but I believe someone's been *playing* ghosts.
And that same someone could have put your
shower cap or whatever it was on the statue,
couldn't they?'

'Well ...' Mrs Mackie said doubtfully.
'I'm not sure about that.'

We left her wondering, and before long
we all fell asleep – even the teachers. When
Fleur nudged me awake we were just pulling into our first stopping place – a large
motorway garage and restaurant.

'Let's get out quickly and be first in the
food queue!' she said, jumping up, and
then she turned back to me and added
in an excited whisper, 'Guess what! Miss
Hermitage has been asleep with her head
on Mr Lloyd's shoulder!'

Smiling broadly at them as we went by,
Fleur and I shuffled off the coach.

'What are you two Cheshire cats grinning
at?' Mr Lloyd asked.

'Nothing ... nothing,' we muttered,
grinning all the more.

He came and stood behind us in the food
queue. 'Who do you think put the knickers
on the statue, Mr Lloyd?' Fleur asked.

He shook his head. 'I really haven't given
it a lot of thought.' He looked at us through
narrowed eyes, smiling. 'Who do you two
think it was, then?'

'Oh, we all reckon it must have been the ghost,' Fleur said airily.

'Ghost?' he said. 'No, I really don't think so.'

'Well, not a real ghost – just the person who did those other things in our dorm who was pretending to be a ghost,' I said.

He laughed. 'Oh no, it wasn't them,' he said.

Fleur and I looked at each other. 'Were you the ghost then, Mr Lloyd?' she asked. 'Buy you a cup of coffee if you tell us!'

He winked. 'As you seem to be able to keep secrets, I'll tell you.' He bent over and whispered, 'Mrs Mackie is the ghost. She does it every year!'

We stared at him in amazement.

'Really?!'

'Cross my heart. She likes to play a joke on her new first-years; it's her little holiday turn. Don't tell anyone, will you?'

'Course not!' we said, making elaborate crosses of our heart.

'She'll want to do it again next year, you see.'

Mr Lloyd had another surprise for us later that day. Eventually, thankfully, we got off the coach and on to the boat home, where he bought everyone a lemonade (the teachers had something stronger) and then announced that he and Miss Hermitage were engaged.

'And we're getting married in September,' Miss Hermitage said, while we all oohed and aahed.

'Will we be able to come to the wedding?' Erica asked.

'Not *all*, I'm afraid,' Miss Hermitage said.

'Perish the thought,' Mr Lloyd said.

'Will you want any bridesmaids?' Cerise asked eagerly. 'Because I've already got this lovely dress, you see. It's only been worn once and ...'

'I've got two younger sisters who'll want to be bridesmaids,' Miss Hermitage interrupted, 'but thank you all the same, Cerise.'

Her face fell. 'But Mummy says I look a picture and ...'

'Cerise!' Erica called. 'Isn't it time that you went to get ready. You want to be looking your best for you-know-what, don't you?'

'Ooh, yes!' she said, running off happily.

The ferry company was a different one from the one we'd come out on, so there wasn't a disco or anything, and because the tide was against us, or perhaps we were just very tired, it seemed to take much longer. We amused ourselves filling in the small spaces on Mouse's plaster leg which hadn't been written on, completing our log books and deciding what we were going to have to eat when we got home.

'Have you enjoyed yourselves?' Mrs Taylor asked when she came round to collect our log books. 'You've all taken to skiing really well.'

We all said yes, we really *had* enjoyed ourselves.

'My best holiday ever,' I said. I sighed. 'I just wish I could have been a bit better at skiing.'

'We can't all be good at everything, Mickey,' she said.

'I don't want to be good at everything, I just want to be good at something,' I explained.

'Well, I think we've already discovered that it's not maths,' she said, 'but who knows, perhaps next term you'll find your forte.'

She moved on. 'What's forte?' I asked Fleur. 'And if I find one do I want it?'

'Your forte is your talent – something you're really good at,' she told me.

'See! You even know meanings of words and I don't!'

'Well, I would do. It's a French word and my mum's French – remember?'

'So she is!' I said. Remembering things obviously wasn't my forte either.

At Dover, exciting things were happening: Su was found locked in one of the loos, being sick; Jasbir discovered she was carrying someone else's luggage – she'd gone to the wrong rack and picked up a soft bag identical to hers – so Mr Lloyd had to get an announcement put over the tannoy; Mouse couldn't go up the gangplank properly so a special little fork lift truck thing arrived for her and Cerise appeared wearing disco glitter and a ton of hair gel ready for her photo call and was sent to 'have a jolly good wash!' by Mrs Mackie.

Eventually we all got through Customs (to our disappointment, no one thought we were international jewel thieves, but just waved us through without a glance) and Mouse disappeared with her mum and dad – they'd come down to collect her in the car to make the last bit of travelling easier.

The rest of us stood round in the big hall waiting to be given instructions and looking for Jane and the photographer and pretending we weren't. We hadn't dared tell Mrs Mackie she was coming. There had been enough fuss when the camera team came to the school; she hadn't got over *that* yet.

'Suppose she's gone to the wrong port!' Cerise said. She bit her lip worriedly. 'Do you think Mrs Mackie will let us call in at Folkestone on the way home, just in case?'

'I rather doubt it,' Annabel said. 'Anyway, she's only some sort of soap star, after all. Who wants to be in the stupid photographs anyway?'

'Me!' Cerise said, just as we all said, 'Cerise does!'

The hall we were waiting in was huge, and people arriving were all mixed in with people departing, so it was difficult to see what was going on.

'I think I'll just go over and stand by the door,' Cerise said anxiously, 'and see if I can see her in the car park.'

'Mrs Mackie said we're not to get separated from each other!' Alice called. 'We're all to wait here until everyone's through from Customs.'

'Oh, I'll just . . .' Cerise began, and then she turned suddenly and saw Jane – blonde hair everywhere and leather coat over her shoulders – hurrying through the big double doors at the end, accompanied by a man with three cameras around his neck.

'Hi! Oh, hi everyone!' she called, and Cerise gave a little skip of joy and then began running eagerly towards her.

The trouble was, she was so eager to get there that she didn't look where she

124

was going and didn't see that there was a leather suitcase right in her path. With a crash and a scream she fell over. And didn't get up again.

Alice ran to get Miss Hermitage, who fetched a first-aid man. We gathered round a white-faced and whimpering Cerise – Jane gathered, too, although I could see she was most put out because no one was taking any notice of her.

'Could one of you go back to my room and ask them to bring a stretcher,' the first-aid man said after feeling Cerise's leg gently.

'Is she just winded?' Miss Hermitage asked.

'No, I'm afraid she's broken her leg!' the first-aid man said – and wondered why we all shrieked.

'I couldn't believe it!' Fleur said later, when we were on the coach with grumpy Mr Johnson driving us the last bit of our journey home. 'Fancy breaking her leg then!'

'Trust her to finish the holiday in spectacular style,' I said.

'Wonder if she'll have a pink plaster cast put on it . . .'

I yawned and sighed. 'Going away's been really good fun, hasn't it? Now we've nothing else to look forward to.'

'We've got next term,' Fleur said. 'Something exciting's bound to happen.'

'Maybe I'll even discover what I'm good at,' I said thoughtfully. Well, a girl can only hope . . .

A Selected List of Fiction from Mammoth

☐	416 13972 8	**Why the Whales Came**	Michael Morpurgo £2.50
☐	7497 0034 3	**My Friend Walter**	Michael Morpurgo £2.50
☐	7497 0035 1	**The Animals of Farthing Wood**	Colin Dann £2.99
☐	7497 0136 6	**I Am David**	Anne Holm £2.50
☐	7497 0139 0	**Snow Spider**	Jenny Nimmo £2.50
☐	7497 0140 4	**Emlyn's Moon**	Jenny Nimmo £2.25
☐	7497 0344 X	**The Haunting**	Margaret Mahy £2.25
☐	416 96850 3	**Catalogue of the Universe**	Margaret Mahy £1.95
☐	7497 0051 3	**My Friend Flicka**	Mary O'Hara £2.99
☐	7497 0079 3	**Thunderhead**	Mary O'Hara £2.99
☐	7497 0219 2	**Green Grass of Wyoming**	Mary O'Hara £2.99
☐	416 13722 9	**Rival Games**	Michael Hardcastle £1.99
☐	416 13212 X	**Mascot**	Michael Hardcastle £1.99
☐	7497 0126 9	**Half a Team**	Michael Hardcastle £1.99
☐	416 08812 0	**The Whipping Boy**	Sid Fleischman £1.99
☐	7497 0033 5	**The Lives of Christopher Chant**	Diana Wynne-Jones £2.50
☐	7497 0164 1	**A Visit to Folly Castle**	Nina Beachcroft £2.25